FAILURE TO THRIVE

MEGHAN LAMB

Failure to Thrive

ISBN-13: 978-1-954899-98-8
ISBN-10: 1-954899-98-X

Cover design by Mike Corrao

www.apocalypse-party.com

Printed in the U.S.A

FAILURE TO THRIVE

You need to know what once was there, or you will never notice anything. You'll likely just drive through it, up the steep curve of the mountain, on the new highway, not knowing there's an old highway—paint-sprayed and cracked, behind the trees—that had to be abandoned.

The whole thing looks like hills and brush.

Some bits of former walls.

A couple houses standing—still—among the empty, flattened plots.

A strangely vacant layered grade that seems too steep to build upon.

A gated graveyard for a church that was knocked down.

*

You need to park along the graveyard, by the clearing in the trees.

Follow the dirt footpath that takes you past the gate's edge, down the hill.

There is an old green garden hose that you can use to scale down it if the mud is too thick, or the snow too deep.

You should try to go in winter, when the snow is deep, because when you come to the base, the open vent between the stones, you'll see the branches of the trees are covered in a sort of frozen, feathered mist, collecting from the vent, the drifts of steam.

*

The steam comes from the fire underneath the ground—inside what was a mine, beneath what was a town—that has been burning over fifty years, that will burn for two hundred more, long after everyone who lived in this town—when it was a town—is dead.

*

There is a whole world pouring from the vent, a world made of heat.

Go in the winter, you will see the sharp change in the atmosphere.

The snow just stops.

The moss stays green.

The air feels tropical.

A gust of pale fog.

A humid sulfur smell.

*

Another garden hose—this one more faded—coils from a tree before the mouth from which the pale fog is pouring. Like someone was attempting to get right down over—into—it. Someone who had a need to know the feeling of the fire.

*

That is all you need to know and that is all there is to see. Now, you can get back on the new highway and drive on through the other mountain towns—the small white houses, seafoam panels, gold-capped steeples, and the rust-bright trickle of a creek—where people are still living.

I
THE LONELY COLD

It is all weighted with absence.
Not even there if you blink too often.

—Harry Humes, "Pennsylvania Coal Town"

Olivia watches the light move from the window to the mirror, making stripes of warmth across the bedroom floor. She has a rule: when the stripes reach the mirror, she will get out of bed. She watches as the light moves toward the mirror's edge. She waits.

She licks her fingertips and puts two fingers in her mouth. Her hand is warm and soft and tastes like pink. She listens for the sound of bedsprings creaking. She listens for the sound of coughing, muffled footsteps.

There is an order:

bedsprings

coughing

muffled footsteps

door shuts

water runs

door shuts again

more footsteps

then, she gets up.

She sucks her fingers harder and the strands of light stretch farther like they're fingers stroking down and down her throat. She doesn't hear the bedsprings or the coughing. She hears a bird perched by the window. She hears another bird call in the distance.

Cooroo
    coo coo
Cooroo
    coo coo
Cooroo
    coo coo
the window bird says.

The bird in the distance says
Coo Roo
    coo
Coo Roo
    coo.
Olivia thinks, soon she'll hear the bedsprings say, crr-creak. But the bird gives one last coo coo, then flies away.

*

This is how the morning usually begins, since David left: she hears the footsteps, gets up, goes into the kitchen. Emily stands with her elbows propped against the counter. She stands there, looking out the window. She wears a blue nightgown with thin white stripes like the slatted lines the window makes. She says something like, maybe we should let the light in.

Olivia wears a white nightgown with light green and yellow flowers. She pretends the green flowers are leaves. That is the color leaves should be. She has a pack of cards with different words and pictures. The green card is a picture of a leaf.

Emily looks out the window and fingers the ends of her hair.

When the morning is how it should be, she then turns and says, good morning, sunshine. Sometimes, when she says this, the sun is making shine. Sometimes, it's not. Sometimes, it's just a thing she says.

Olivia sits at the table and looks at the tablecloth. The cloth is this shiny stiff fabric with red and white squares. The squares are all covered with ants, but the ants are not real—like Emily tells her—not alive, Olivia. They are just drawings. She touches the drawings of ants while Emily makes coffee. To make coffee, she pours blackish powder into a black bowl. After awhile, the pot makes a noise like your stomach when it's hungry. Coffee tastes like boiling mud. It smells like burning dirt.

Olivia gets the small bowls from the low shelf, gets the small spoons from the drawer, the milk box from the fridge, and the cereal box from the pantry. She scoops the cereal into the bowl using a plastic spoon they keep inside the box for scooping til it's empty. Olivia waits for Emily to pour the milk. She hasn't figured out a way to do it without spilling.

She eats her cereal while Emily drinks coffee. When her cereal bowl is empty, she counts all the ants. 18, 19, 20, now 21: the numbers 2 and 1, the numbers of how many years she is.

There are 24 ants on the table cloth. She wishes there were 25. She doesn't count out loud. She counts with quiet voices in her head.

*

Olivia knows the order of her mornings, but sometimes the weather has a way of making time seem strange. Like when the clouds begin to build when Emily tells her, good morning, sunshine, and she has a headache and the kitchen light feels too sharp. That's when she goes back to her room to check the schedule. She can't control the clouds. Her schedule always stays the same.

7:30 am - 7:45 am	Up
7:45 am - 8:15 am	Eat
8:15 am - 8:30 am	Clean
8:30 am - 8:35 am	Med
8:35 am - 8:45 am	Brush teeth
8:45 am - 9:00 am	Dress
9:00 am - 10:00 am	Play
10:00 am - 11:00 am	Words
11:00 am - 11:30 am	TV
11:30 am - 12:00 pm	Cook
12:00 pm - 12:30 pm	Eat
12:30 pm - 1:00 pm	Clean

Olivia looks at the black square clock beside her bed. The glowing numbers on the clock are green. The numbers on the clock say 7:26. Olivia watches until they say 7:27.

She looks at all the pictures on her chart. Emily printed the pictures on the computer. They are cut-out squares she covered in a shiny see-through sheet. The backs of all the squares are tiny squares of velcro.

She looks at the sleeves of her yellow and green-flowered nightgown. The scalloped edges of the sleeves are gray. The nightgown is old, like she is old, like David said: too old to suck your hand. She looks at the gray while she sucks on her fingers.

She looks at the picture for Up. It shows an outline of a bed, an upright arrow. The bed is drawn from the perspective of a person looking at it from the front, the baseboard facing outward. She imagines this ghost of a person looks down on her as she fulfills her routine, this strange person who sees her whole life as a series of black and white squares. She imagines this person is also a simply-drawn outline. The person's voice speaks like an outline, a silent, it's time to get up, now. Get up.

She hears the silent outline of this voice as she looks at the clock and sees the numbers now say 7:30.

*

Olivia keeps sucking on her fingers. She makes tiny little whispered slurping sounds. Other people do not like these sounds, she knows. If no one hears her, they will not tell her to stop what she is doing.

She sucks on her fingers because she likes the sound. The sound makes a tingle that runs from her tongue through her head. The tingle makes her head, her hand, her mouth all feel connected. It feels good to be reminded she is all one body.

Olivia sucks on her hand until she starts to forget this, until she feels shivering and sharpness where her mouth can't reach.

She listens to her mouth go

Shh

    Sss

Shh

    Sss

Shh

    Sss

Shh

    Sss

Shh

    Sss

Shh

The sharpness softens and the shivers become warm. Each finger of her hand is warm inside her mouth. She tastes the flow of blood beneath her skin. She listens to the rhythms, to the movements she is making.

After awhile, her hand begins to taste a little sour. She opens her mouth and she looks at her hand in the light. Her fingers are whiteish and soggy and speckled with red. They look the way they always looked when she took off her gloves.

The gloves are blue and rubbery. They make her hands taste sour. They leave white powder on her hands that makes them hurt. She always had to wear the gloves when David was around. When David lived here, he would always make her wear the gloves.

She imagines the blue of the gloves as she closes her eyes. She breathes in for a moment with her mouth wide-open. She buries the wet of her hand in her lap and she places her other hand into her mouth. She thinks, this is our house, now. Our own house.

*

They live together in a small gray single-story house. Their bedrooms run along the same straight wall. Olivia sleeps in the back room, which looks out onto the woods. Emily sleeps in the front room, which looks out into the open. The middle room was sometimes David's room. Now, David's room is where she keeps the CDs, books, and bags of things.

The bedrooms line the right side of the house. The left side of the house is for the kitchen and the living room. The kitchen's on the back side near Olivia. There is a picture window by the kitchen sink. That's the window that Emily opens when she's doing dishes, where steam rises and absorbs the cool scent of trees.

The living room feels uneasy no matter what Emily does with the light. When the curtains are drawn—which they usually are— the room is dark and stiff. Small claws of light fight through the curtains, cutting through the floor boards. When she opens the curtains, dust shimmers up into the air. The knotted floors look treacherous, like bruised and blistered skin. The walls look dry, blank surfaces of cracked, unblinking white.

Their house sits off a graveled sliver of a road that curves in shaky lines along the edges of the hills. The only people that drive through this road live on another road that runs back through the woods, into the mountains.

This road is not a road someone drives onto accidentally.

This road is the start of a long line that only leads further away into nothing.

*

In Olivia's room, the lines of light have reached all the way to the mirror. The numbers on the clock are 7:56. Her stomach is making the sound of the coffee machine. Her mouth burns with the tingling from her hand.

Outside of her room, it is winter. The trees and the mountains are no longer green and the road is not pebbled with gray. Everything has been changed by the weather and everything is now white. When Olivia takes her hand out of her mouth for a moment, the room becomes quiet. She then hears a deep metal groaning from inside the pipes, the slow crackle of ice in the gutters.

She doesn't hear the creaking of the bedsprings. She doesn't hear the coughing or the footsteps. She doesn't hear the sound of running faucets. She doesn't hear the sound of drawers or cabinets being shut.

She doesn't hear the clinking clank of dishes. She doesn't hear the sudden sound of something being dropped, the sound of hissing breath and shit, shit, shit, shit, shit.

She doesn't hear the sound of Hello? Speaking. Or, Hello? No. Not interested.

It is 8:05. If she were in the kitchen, she would count the ants. She would touch them, one by one, until she knew she'd touched them all. She'd take her bowl and spoon to the sink. She'd make sure any crumbled bits of cereal were swept away.

The number 24 has never seemed quite right. She knows that someday, when she counts them, she will count to 25. She knows there's something more to life than what she sees and hears. She knows there's always something hiding just beneath the surface.

*

It is 8:30. It is time to take her medicine. Olivia looks at the medicine square on her chart. The symbol for Med is an open mouth without a face and an arrow that points to three pills that look like they are floating in space.

Olivia opens her mouth like the mouth in the picture. Her breath tastes dry. Her hands are red. She swallows hard.

It is 8:35. It is time to brush her teeth and then get dressed. She thinks about what she would wear, what Emily would wear. She has a pale yellow shirt with small white daisies on it. They are prints of a daisy, the same daisy image repeated again and again. She always wears a pair of green pants with the shirt. She also wears a pair of daisy-printed socks that match. There are 47 daisies on the shirt. There are 22 daisies on both of her socks, or 11 on each.

Olivia has 13 shirts, 4 pairs of pants, 4 pairs of shoes, 12 pairs of socks, and 16 pairs of underwear.

Almost everything Emily wears is pale blue or gray. She likes to wear the different colors of the sky. The flash card for Blue is the sky, but the sky can be gray, or light blue, or dark blue with gray clouds, or light yellowish-gray, so light gray it becomes almost white.

The card for White is snow, but snow is also many colors. White-gray. White-blue. White-yellow. White-pink, even, sometimes. One time, when she was outside playing in the snow, her nose began to bleed, and it dripped down into the white. She remembers the taste of blood when she sucks on her hand. She remembers the millions of colors that she cannot name.

*

When the morning is how it should be and Olivia brushes her teeth and gets dressed, she stands before her bedroom mirror and looks at the room through the mirror's reflection. She hears Emily moving in the bathroom. She hears something spraying, sprit, sprit, sprit.

The fluttering of wings of vapor in the air, the wings Emily waves with the flat of her hand as she comes up behind in the mirror. She helps brush Olivia's hair, braid Olivia's hair, wrap the pink rubber band all around with a snip-snap, and kisses Olivia's head and says, all done.

Olivia thinks, all done, as she sees the clock says 9:00. She knows that it is time to work on Words. The room is filled with filtered blueish sunlight. She looks at the light and she thinks, ok, now, all done. She puts a finger back into her mouth. This time, instead of sucking, she begins to bite.

The shadows of branches brush their tips against the window. She stares at the space of the window where the line of light shines through. She imagines the limbs of the trees stretching farther, the contrast of light getting sharper, the outlines of shapes getting darker and darker until they pierce straight through the glass. She imagines the rush of the wind. She imagines the bright gleaming shatter, imagines the wind now not only a sound, but a cold that surrounds her, fills everything, swallows the breath from her throat.

*

Emily says good morning sunshine looking good look at the chart ok what do we do first let me help you good job no Olivia remember we are done we are all finished now ok Olivia look at the chart again time out Olivia five minutes when the clock says 9:07 when the clock says 9:12 when the clock says 9:15 the clock says 10:00 the clock says 10:15 look at the clock what does the clock say now look at the chart look at me look at me ok now you need to wash your hands you need to take your shoes off wash your hands look at me when the clock says 12:05 ok ok look at the chart what do we do now good job ok now it's time to wash your hands to help me clean the table help me clean the chair time out the clock says 1:03 the clock says 1:05 if you do that again time out the time is 1:15 ok what did you do what are you doing go look at the chart what are you doing ok that is not ok what are you doing help me that is not ok Olivia.

*

Olivia bites down harder on her hand. The shiver in her head becomes a shot of pain. It's like the feeling when she sees bright spots of colors from the light, shuts her eyes, presses down her eyelids, and watches the colors explode.

Her stomach hurts. She has to pee. She holds it. Shifts in bed. The springs creak. Her ears prick. Then nothing. She looks at the clock. It's 9:17. She doesn't like this number. One plus seven equals eight, not nine. She watches the clock and she nibbles her hand til it says 9:18, then she bites.

She hears

Cooroo

    coo coo

Cooroo

    coo coo

Cooroo

    coo coo

The bird is nearby. It is probably calling from Emily's window.

Cooroo

    coo coo

Cooroo

coo coo

The bird waits quietly. Olivia closes her eyes and waits. No one calls back.

*

When David lived with them, she wore the gloves all day. It felt wrong to have blue hands instead of pink. The gloves tasted like soap. She couldn't spit them off her hands and when she tried to take them off, he told her Bad, he called her, Bad Olivia.

If David had a pack of cards that named things, Bad would be a picture of Olivia without her gloves.

If Olivia's pack of flashcards had a card called David, it would show an outline of the gloves, an arrow pointing to the word Bad.

When wearing the gloves, she couldn't feel the tingle in her head. She couldn't turn the sharpness in her head to pinkish softness. Her head and her hands were caught up in the gloves. She felt she couldn't feel them. She felt drawn on, outlined, sectioned off from herself.

She felt her head get hot. She bit things, hit things, hid things. David punished her for biting, hitting, took more things away. When he punished her, he called her Bad. She knew that being Bad meant she'd keep losing things as David moved them wherever he wanted.

Sometimes, when David was away, Emily took the gloves off. She said nothing. She just took them off and looked away. She looked out of the window, made dinner, washed dishes, and covered the sound of Olivia's hands with the clinking of plates and the hiss of the running water. She kept the gloves folded inside of a napkin inside of a drawer. She always put the gloves back on before David came home.

*

Olivia shifts back and forth in bed. It is 10:45 and she can't hold it anymore. She folds back the covers. She follows the line of light to her bathroom. She uses the bathroom attached to her room, with the pink tub and the blue-green floor.

She closes her eyes when she pees. She feels like something's getting sucked out. She presses her slimy red hands into her stomach. The box light flickers yellow-white, white, yellow-white, like lightning. She stands wobbly. She washes her hands with three pumps of the vanilla soap.

She opens the drawer as quietly as she can. She touches Emily's hair clips. She opens them and presses on their teeth. She bites the insides of her cheeks. She sniffles. Puts them back inside the drawer. She closes the drawer and in her head, she whispers, Emily?

The branches tap against the glass.

Emily?

She hears a creak, but it's only the branches outside.

Emily?

The branches creak and creak. The wind makes little whimpers.

Emily?

The whimpers fade away to whispers.

The wind dies down. The branches still. The room is shades of yellow-gray. The lines of shadows brighten and the house falls silent.

*

Emily has a soft voice colors yellow hair green eyes soft freckles on her arms soft speaking when she gives directions slow voice when she speaks she reads soft stories skin smells soft like lotion like vanilla soap like brushing hair soft hands soft fingers like she buys soap buys CDs buys DVDs she doesn't make Olivia eat foods she doesn't like she doesn't make Olivia wear gloves unless her hands get red her eyes are red she cries smells like smoke smells forgetting where she put things how she leaves things how she takes Olivia to doctors take her medicine take care of her how looking out the window sad she's speaking on the phone how she is lonely how she is alone how people make no sense how she does things now that make no sense to Olivia like losing track of things.

*

It is 11:30. She pictures what she would be doing if this day were as it should be. On a typical day at this time, she puts away her flash cards and wipes off the table. Emily sets the dishes and turns on the gas stove. The stove goes, click, click, click, tic, tic, tic, tic, whoosh. She hears the sound of boiling and she pours the macaroni or she scoops the can of white or yellow soup. Then (this is her favorite part) she gets to watch the bubbles pop. The white or yellow bubbles pop, pop, pop inside the pot.

Instead, she's popping bubbles in her mouth. She runs wet fingers through her thin dry strands of hair. She bristles all the edges, thinks of snow and ice and mountains filled with holes.

She thinks of all the things that fall inside the holes. She thinks of being trapped. She thinks of standing, staring up into a hole of sun. She feels brittle. Hair falls out into her hand. She thinks of all the tall trees growing on and on, and on, and on, and on, and on, and on, and on, forever.

*

They used to live in town. In town, they had a light blue house. In town, the front yard was a broken sidewalk and a slab of concrete. In town, the backyard was a dead tree, tall grass, and a chain-link fence. In town, behind the fence was mud, and stones, and train tracks.

She liked to sit beside a crack inside the sidewalk. It was always moving. Emily said, ants. The crack was a shimmer the ants poured themselves in and out of. Their movements sparkled like a many-bodied stream.

Emily explained, they live beneath the sidewalk. Like we live inside this house beneath another family.

Everybody seems to live on top of someone else, she thought.

She nibbled on her fingers as she watched the ants.

*

The train was loud at night. She slept beneath the covers with her head beneath the pillow and her hands clasped to her ears. The train just moaned as loudly as it wanted to. She felt her world being buried underneath its sound.

*

It is 1:00. Lunch would be over now. The table would be clean. They'd move on to page two of Olivia's schedule. Olivia thinks, Emily, again. She thinks, come help me, but she doesn't come. It's time to change the schedule.

She waits until the clock says 1:01. She shifts in bed. The springs creak and she waits, but it's just her. She stands and walks along the line of light and takes the schedule down. She puts it in a plastic folder-shelf that's stuck onto the wall. She takes the second schedule from the shelf and hangs it up. She looks and thinks that she has no idea what to do now.

The schedule says

1:00 pm - 1:30 pm	Play
1:30 pm - 2:00 pm	TV
2:00 pm - 3:00 pm	Walk
3:00 pm - 4:30 pm	Play
4:30 pm - 5:00 pm	Words
5:30 pm - 5:45 pm	Clean
5:45 pm - 5:50 pm	Med
5:50 pm - 6:15 pm	Cook
6:15 pm - 6:45 pm	Eat
6:45 pm - 7:00 pm	Clean
7:00 pm - 8:00 pm	Bath
8:00 pm - 8:15 pm	PJs
8:15 pm - 8:30 pm	Brush Teeth
8:30 pm - 9:00 pm	Read Book
9:00 pm	Sleep

She feels the way she felt when David lived with them, when Emily took off the gloves when David wasn't looking. She knew he couldn't see she wasn't wearing them. She also knew that somehow, he would sense that something wasn't right. He would get angry when he came home. He'd get mad that something wasn't cleaned, or something wasn't clean enough, or something wasn't there. Or he'd get mad at nothing, really. He'd just sit and look at nothing like he wasn't really there and there was nothing there to look at.

Olivia looks at the schedule like there's nothing there. It's already 1:15 and she has not done anything. She has not

cleaned the table

eaten lunch

made lunch

worked on her words

gone for a walk

watched TV

put on day clothes

brushed her teeth

swallowed her medicine

cleaned off the kitchen

eaten breakfast

watched Emily drink her coffee

watched Emily look out the window

heard her say, good morning, sunshine

or heard bed springs creaking from Emily's room.

She watches as a spider scurries up the wall. Its hurried movements make her realize how fast her heart is beating. It crawls into a corner where the wall becomes the ceiling, where it's spinning little gauzy knots of dust-collecting shine. She sees something twitch that's tangled in the knot. She squints. She twitches and her stomach clutches. She gets back in bed. Her legs get tangled in the sheets. The spider lunges. She looks down. She looks away. Her stomach feels like a long-forgotten basement.

*

The people came too close when they lived in the town. They looked at her. She tried to look away. There was something in their looks that caught and held her. Teeth. Their toothy faces, she thought. Somehow sharp and soft at the same time.

At night, she watched the porch swing sway. The curtains billowed. Emily brought in a glass of water, tucked her into bed. She told her they would move into the mountains. We will live in our own house, she said. She smiled when she said, our own.

*

It is 2:00. She should be getting dressed to go outside. She should be putting on her snow coat and her snow boots. She should go find her purple coat with the white stripes along the sleeves. She should go find her purple polka dotted scarf and cap and gloves.

She should be sitting at the table while Emily puts on her gray-blue hooded sweatshirt, bright blue jacket, light blue scarf, and white-gray cap. She should put on her coat and wait for Emily to help her with the tricky zipper and the tiny buttons on the wrists. She should wait, holding in her breath while Emily puts on her scarf, winding her neck and mouth into a warm protective nest.

She should be walking through the trees until they reach the gap that overlooks the mountains on one side, their old town on the other. They should be passing their green water bottle back and forth. They should be getting cold. They should be going back inside to get warm.

But Olivia can't get warm because she did not get cold. She can't go back inside because she did not go outside. She can't go outside without putting on her winter clothes. She cannot put on all her winter clothes without the help of Emily.

She falls asleep. She dreams about the winter sky. She dreams that she is standing in the clearing, looking at the clouds with Emily. She dreams the clouds begin to slowly separate themselves, their outlines breaking into small shapes, drifting off into the distance.

*

Our own house in the woods the mountains by the town the other people that we do not need like how we need things how you need your room your bed your schedule but the trees the mountains they do not belong to you do not belong to anyone you walk along the path you cannot see beneath the snow your boot scrapes then you see that there are many things the trees are green beneath they look the same but wet the rain the snow the wind the lighting strikes the trees we see them down we see them down like bodies down like you live down inside your body like you sleep inside your body in your own room in your own house in the woods the mountains in your body like you could be struck by lightning if you stood outside your house and stood and waited long enough for rain.

*

When she wakes, the room turns gold, the curtains haloed. She knows soon it will be dark. She swallows, gasping, like she swallowed something sharp. She gasps. Emily. Emily. She looks around the room. She listens. Nothing. Ears and eyes open to everything.

She sucks in breath. The wind blows at the window. She gets up. The bedsprings shriek. She doesn't care. She's walking back and forth across the room.

The wind is getting louder and the sun begins to set.

She paces, turning.

Shadows darken.

She sits down.

She stares into the ceiling.

She begins to scream.

She's screaming.

She just screams.

She screams and screams and screams until she can't hear what she's screaming.

*

Then, she stops.

The room is dark and nothing's happening.

She thinks, nothing has happened. If I stay, nothing will happen.

She stands up. Her throat is sore. Her legs are numb. They feel frozen. There's a silver line of light that forms a pathway to the door.

28

*

Today, the sky is like the ocean, thinks Emily. She has never seen the ocean. She's seen pictures. She would like to go someday, to see some deep blue arctic ocean. She imagines what she longs to see: blue waves with islands of white ice.

She walks with David, looking up into the ocean of the sky. The trees have shed their leaves. The sky flows all around them. They climb up a steep ledge through the hills, their feet slick on the snow. She glances at her feet, then at the sky, then at her feet.

She turns to David. Have you ever seen the ocean?

Like, in real life? He says, one time. I don't remember. I was young.

That's a shame, says Emily. That is a shame, she thinks. In many ways, it's worse to know you've seen something you can't recall.

They reach the ledge that the town calls Lovers' Leap. They look at one another, faces reddened, breathing vapor clouds. The clouds drift through the air between them, lingering in place of words. Emily blows into her hands, then cups them to the edges of her face.

They stand between the bare trees, looking at the town: a quilt of faded teal, rust-brown, patched with clapboard crusts. Long lines of ancient gravestones, rising up the incline of a hill. Some toppled, like they might descend upon the not-yet-dead. Black smoke is rising from a burning pile on a hill. She thinks about the black smoke blending with the clouds. She thinks about the black smoke melting her imagined islands, sinking her imagined ships, dulling the waters of her ocean.

I do still love the way it looks, from here. David exhales.

All the colors? She says, flatly.

David says, no. Just the hills. When you look at the houses, close-up, they look like they're falling down, but from a distance, it looks like the hills are holding them in place.

She thinks, he sees the good in things, and maybe that is what she needs.

She says, you see the good in things. That's why I love you.

*

At the apartment, they strip off their wet clothes one piece at a time: an awkward, tripping over dance into the bedroom.

David lays his clothes out on the radiator. They'll get fried, says Emily.

Don't care, says David. It's just clothes.

They crawl under the covers and they touch each other. She rubs her still-red cheeks into David's still-damp beard. He smells like coal. She coughs. He kisses her nose and it tickles and she laughs. Her cold feet toss across the sheets.

*

I want the one that's burnt, she tells him when he's making grilled cheese. She smiles at the sound of metal scraping crackled bits. He flips a darkened sandwich on the plate she likes, the small one with the blue dots and the glaze that looks like sprinkled pepper.

They sit beside the window, eating, looking at the backyard. It's a concrete slab, a patch of dead grass, and a patch of mud. A silver metal gate quivers in waves against the wind. A fast food wrapper flaps against it like a clumsy paper plane.

David makes coffee after dinner. He works 10-6 two counties over at the plant. The cleaning crew, a decent enough job. As good as he could get, as close as he could get, at least for now. The drive's an hour and a half, two hours on a snowy day.

Emily takes his plate, hands him his cup. He kisses her and sips. He says, I love you, and she says, I love you too.

She washes each plate with three squirts of soap she wrings out from the sponge. She runs the water over them for 12 seconds. She counts. That is her favorite number, 12. She's turning 21, this year. She wonders if that is bad luck, or good.

Emily dresses for her job. She wears the store's black polo shirt. She wears the khakis with the zipper she clips with a safety pin. She pulls her hair back, clips it, turning back and forth before the mirror. She brushes her teeth violently. Spits blood into the sink.

*

She walks along the street that wraps around the town. The train tracks in the distance. The abandoned textile mills. Beyond the mills, the slopes of coal, speckled with small, dry greenish shrubs of what were—once—or what are—almost—forests. The churches are still beautiful. She passes by the pale stone cathedral with its crown-like copper towers. The theater is still beautiful: a blonde brick, carved stone block, a silver awning, and a marquee filled with broken bulbs. She passes by the house that burned into its own gradation. Attic: white-gray. Second floor: dark gray. The first floor: almost black. A clothes line still hangs in the backyard of that house. Old fashioned wood pins, little naked bodies frozen to the wire.

She crosses through the back lot of the high-rise. Her mother lives there, somewhere on the sixth floor. She thinks, poor woman. In that building. In that little room. That's how she's come to think about her mother, now. Poor woman.

*

The manager is standing outside, smoking.

She nods.

Emily nods.

Cold.

Yep.

Want one?

Sure.

They stand there, breathing smoke.

They stare into a brick wall with a mural of the town. The snow beneath the wall is clouded with a mist of faded seafoam paint.

Emily coughs.

Her manager coughs and she rubs her eyes.

Emily coughs, again.

They breathe in, try to clear their lungs.

*

When Emily was young, her mother walked her by the mural wall. The seafoam paint was peeling even then. Her mother looked at Emily and pointed to the wall. Her mother told her, this is where we live.

*

On Sunday afternoons, they go to David's parents' house for dinner. They file through the kitchen, filling up their plates with food. Steamed peas and sweet corn. Scalloped cheese potatoes. Casseroles and crescent rolls. A pot of coffee. A cooler of beer.

David sits with his brothers, yelling at the game. His older uncles gather in the back room, where they sit and smoke. The women shuffle through the background, taking dirty plates. The sink piles. Kitchen walls absorb the humid scents, the panels peeling.

Emily drifts among the women, following their movements, but she doesn't speak to them unless she's spoken to.

The house is filled with albums, tables, walls of family photos. In the living room, there is a wall devoted just to David: An array that starts—top corner—his first day of kindergarten—and ends—bottom corner—with his graduation.

*

They sit by the TV at home, their beer cans crushed around the couch. She likes the sound, the cold crack—hiss—of each can as it opens. She's learned to like the sound. She's learned to like the taste of them. She's learned how not to notice how the cans accumulate.

David yawns. He leans in through the long arch of a stretch. His arm encircles her.

He says, hey.

She says, hey.

He repeats, hey.

He kisses her. He tastes like beer, but so does she. She strokes his hair.

His hands move up her shirt, then down her pants. The TV glows.

Their faces, blue-lit, look like aliens, their movements clumsy.

She laughs at him when their jawlines clip together.

She says, hey. She's making fun of how he said it.

David doesn't seem to notice. He keeps kissing through his injury.

Outside, the mountain wind throws itself up against the walls. It blows so hard it sounds like human hands against the window. She thinks, there's something beautiful and treacherous, out there.

She moves in closer so he doesn't need to reach for her.

*

There is the world as it is—as it has always been—for Emily. The world of the town, the mural of the town. She knows it's very sad, the way things have disintegrated. Or, at least, she knows that she should feel sad.

*

Pale teal. Rust. The wind. The falling-down wallpaper. Long walks through the hills. The dingy yards with sun-bleached plastic toys. Neighborhood bars. Sundays with family. Sulfuric-smelling creek. The looming threat of bad—bad teeth, bad-smelling rooms, bad knees, bad back—of getting old.

*

There is the world she imagines her town used to be, the world in the photographs that people like to point to. Yes, there were jobs—then—jobs and money. Pictures of her great-aunts in the mill, surrounded by the silk looms. Long strands. Fairytale spider webs.

The blonde brick movie theater. Healthy children riding bikes. New papered walls. A thriving lawn. A postcard from the beach. The holidays. A mural, painted in the still-new colors of the town. A backyard filled with people, not with broken toys.

Hard to believe it was the same space. That the old library building was a big department store. That those abandoned buildings were small boutique stores that sold silk stockings and silk dresses. That her uncles packed those same silk garments up in stacks of boxes and delivered them in trucks to grand shops in New York.

*

There is the world of her family before they left, before the high-rise.

Her father on the porch. Her sister in her room.
The TV. Windows cracked. Sounds bleeding into sounds.
Smoke blown out through the cracks.
The metal fan making its slow, stiff revolution.

*

As David pulls out of the driveway, his throat feels tight. A mesh of tensions, like a metal grate that molds around his muscles. As he pulls onto the main road, he feels like the mesh is rattling. He drives through town. He sees the porch light of his parent's home.

He feels the mesh start to disintegrate. He swallows as he turns onto the highway.

He sees other cars, likely driving off to jobs like his. Most likely people like him, from these other neighbor towns. Most likely other guys like him, with ordinary lives. He sees the other ordinary towns. He sees the ways they look the same.

The old brick mills. The churches. Metal bridges. Layered ripples of white hills, the layered lines of road and rail. Quiet darkness and the slow curves of the snow, lit by his headlights. He feels—like he says—they're held together by the hills.

*

The snow melts. Redbuds bloom to leaves to summer. Hills turn lavender, then deep green. Hills feel like they're stretching, yawning fog. They open windows. Emily places the metal fan beside the bed. Their curtains billow, like their lives are flowing into something.

When she walks to work, she sees two girls with long, brown, straggled hair knelt on a side road, drawing hearts with sticks of chalk. One girl wears no shoes and the other wears a pair of pink, cracked plastic mules. Their bare white legs are filled with bruises.

The store is cold and bright. She watches people coming in and out to get their toilet paper, dish soap, bar soaps in 3-packs, their off-brand sodas, frozen burgers, baby wipes, minute rice, cheap sunglasses, cigarette lighters with prints of American flags.

While Emily stocks, she sees teenagers sneak things into their bags. It's usually just packs of snack food. Sometimes blank CDs.

She looks up at them.

They look down like, shit.

She looks back at them like, go on. Who the fuck cares?

*

She lingers over things she never cared about before. She starts to notice, on some level, she's afraid of losing them. Like in the morning, when she stares into her coffee at the hundreds of minute reflected bubbles of herself.

When David walks with her, it bothers him to see her kicking pinecones. He ignores it, the first time. The second and third time, he says, leave it alone. She gets another good kick in, then feels guilty. Her ears follow the pinecone as it scrapes and shivers down the rocks.

*

She lies in bed at night, imagining the ocean.

Isn't that where people go, this time of year?

What people?

Other people.

Why?

They try to fill the ocean with their bodies and the ocean sucks them in.

She imagines the Pacific and Atlantic oceans. Two blue bodies on a map, the unseen borders of her world. She pictures blue veins trickling into the land mass on the map, lengthening, widening, until the land becomes a mesh of tiny islands. She imagines the blue water freezing over. She imagines the town, frozen over, worn old houses fading into sludge, and she imagines the still-lovely buildings freezing into glaciers, crystal palaces preserved forever in their place.

David rolls over, brushes back the damp hair from her shoulders, kisses them. The bristles of his beard brush up against her nipples. She shifts. He pulls up her nightgown. His cock is already out. He pushes in, her legs, her mouth. The hairs around his mouth are wet.

She grabs his shoulders tight. The room begins to smell like sweat.

Her skin feels so hot, on its surface, but so cold somewhere beneath.

The curtains billow.

His breath, rasping. His blue shadowed ribcage.

The fan rattles until it straightens itself out again.

*

How the fuck. David's brothers are hollering at the TV in the bar. How the hell did he miss. That's a routine ground ball. Motherfucker! The fuck do you do that!

Sonofabitch! David slams his now empty beer bottle. The bartender brings him a new one. He drinks it and nods. He looks back up. Come on! He says, Sonofabitch!

He glances down at Emily. She's peeling back the label of her bottle. It peels clean, at first, where condensation has built up, but then it starts to fray. She peels it anyway. The frayed, soft paper edges curl, like long white strips of birch.

His brother hisses as he takes a sip. He makes a smacking sound. He mumble-hisses, that bum in right field. Sips. He always overthrows the cutoff. Sips. Emily hears him mumble something else as all three brothers put their bottles down almost in unison.

She picks the peeled bits of label out from underneath her nails. David looks at her. Stop doing that. You know it bugs me.

She shrugs guiltily, sweeps the bits of peeled label underneath the bar, taps her last cigarette out from the pack.

The bar fades to a low, mumbling growl. David's brother says something about some girl who'll spread her legs for anyone. Emily looks at David to read his reaction. David's face is turned away from her. She scratches at the label.

Motherfuck! More slamming bottles. How the fuck! His brother stands. His bottle almost spills. The fuck you hang a curveball to that guy?

You hang em, they bang em, says David.

Emily looks down.

He looks at her. Sips. Repeats, in a softer tone, you hang em, they bang em.

*

She thinks about the oceans pumped beneath the mountains, veins of thickened water, flowing underneath green waves.

She thinks about the sound of it, the rush of water pumped so hard it splits the layers of the mountains, breaks their bones and makes them bleed.

He lifts her nightgown, nibbles at her lip, mumbles something about her tits, mumbles something about something he wants to do to them, and how she likes it, yes, yes, yes, she does, and she closes her eyes, feels overtaken, feels the edges of the whole world disappear.

She thinks about the sound of the explosion.

She thinks about the sound of the explosion.

She thinks about the sound of the explosion.

She imagines the cold pressure of the silence, both before and after.

*

I had sex 3 days before my period could I be pregnant?

I had sex on my period could I get pregnant yes or no?

My bf and me both had sex. He didn't cum. My period got heavy. Am I still good?

Emily scans the Family Planning online Q and A, hoping to find the answer to the question that she doesn't want to ask. She doesn't find the information that she needs. She types in her own question:

Do you help out with abortions?

*

She hesitates, holding her plate, that night, visiting David's family. She lifts each spoon up for a moment. Then, she sets it down. The room smells strange. The air inside the kitchen feels heavy. She takes two plain dinner rolls. She fills a glass of water.

She says, sorry, when they look at her, seeking an explanation. I don't feel good. I don't know what is wrong.

*

We do not help out with abortions, the website replies.

If you can visit our office, we will refer you to someone who can.

We must request you make sure you are really pregnant.

We must request you make sure this is what you really want to do.

*

Emily finds her mother by a window in the high-rise. She comes up from the side, stepping into the light. She whispers, Ma. Her mother doesn't turn. She says, Hello, Ma. Her mother's head tilts upward in what might be called a nod.

Her mother doesn't turn. Emily moves toward her, slowly, carefully. She stands beside her mother by the window.

What's there? Emily looks.

From here, they can see almost everything.

From here, they have a clear view of the old brick factories.

The boarded windows are a mix of brown and teal wood.

They look like many sets of closed and opened eyes.

Emily hears a woman crying in her room, somewhere. The hallway smells like lukewarm stale soup. A cargo train comes through the tracks beyond the factories. They watch the long line of its many-colored cars.

They listen to its chimes: three sad full-throated cries.

Emily glances at her mother. For a moment, she is almost smiling.

*

On the cold toilet seat, inside the bare white-walled employee restroom, Emily watches the middle line appear. It is a ghostly shadowing, at first, but quickly, it becomes a solid stripe. Firm-lined. Irrevocably blue.

She throws it out, washes her hands, and microwaves a frozen burrito.

21 seconds. She flips it. Then, 21 seconds. Then, 21 seconds again.

She peels the wrapper back. She eats as fast as possible. She swallows numbly even though the middle is still cold.

*

There is the world Emily has always known: the feeling of life flowing through her, coldly and reluctantly. There is the world of the feeling she has, looking at the sky, the trees, the graveyard, and the changing colors of the hills.

Emily knows that there are worlds beyond her little world. There are people that are feeling things within them. But these people and their feelings are unreachable to her. She can't even decipher thoughts of people she can see.

*

The woman at the Family Planning Center doesn't look at Emily. She just hands her a print-off with a circled line. She just keeps asking Emily if she would like a cup of cold water. No, she wouldn't. That will not solve anything.

*

Dusk falls as Emily begins her walk home from the center. She walks by the faded chipping mural of the town. A crazy-looking man is pacing by the mural. He is staring at something he's holding cupped inside his hands.

He calls to Emily. He says, the stones have faces.

What? She says.

Come see them, he says, holding out his hands.

She sees three coal-like pebbles filled with indentations.

He points to the indentations. Here, and here, and here, he says.

She looks back at him, blankly.

He says, look, this is a face. He points again. Here, here, and here, he whispers.

It's a face. A face. The stones have faces.

Emily nods and she continues on her walk.

She looks down at her feet, the many stones she's always trampling.

The many stones, the many faces, held together by the hills.

The many stones she sees each day, but never sees.

They have faces, they have faces, they have faces.

She thinks ok, ok, ok. I fucking get it.

*

Olivia opens the door and the line of light spreads. She looks down the hallway. She looks down at Emily's door. She stands there, for a moment, in the silver beam of light. She stands and looks. The hall is dark. The door is closed.

She listens to the sound of ice inside the pipes. Small scratching sounds, like fingernails trapped behind the walls. She puts a finger in her mouth and looks along the shadowed hall. She steps forward with gentle, careful, patterned movements.

One step. Look down.

Two steps. Look up.

The door. Still closed.

One step. Look down.

Two steps. Look up.

The door. Still closed.

One step. Look down.

Two nibbles on the finger in her mouth.

Two steps. Look up.

One step. Look down.

One long breath.

Look.

The door. Still closed.

She touches the glass knob of Emily's bedroom door. It feels cold beneath her hand. It warms a bit, beneath her touch.

She shivers, switches hands. She puts the doorknob fingers in her mouth.

She tastes the fluids they have channeled through them.

*

David slides along the cold, dark metal curve, crouched on his toes. He runs his blue-gloved hand along the vat, tracing a path. He feels tugging on his harness from outside the vat. A voice. Doing all right in there?

He coughs. Yeah. Doing fine.

His heart pricks at him, quietly. He thinks, don't be a pussy. Strong smells clinging to the mixing blades. Wet clumps of whey.

Dark bluish pools, drips of cleaning chemicals. He shines a flashlight on them. They shine back, there, in the center of the vat.

The blades stand stiff and still, there, on their metal pole, curling down all around it like some starkly gleaming spine. He scrapes the blades. Thick sludge comes loose and slaps down to the metal floor. He can't help feeling he's been swallowed up by something.

He scrapes. He shines his light.

The edges of the blade gleam back.

He thinks, don't think about the blades.

The scraping echoes through the vat.

*

It is his job to clean the blades cause if the blades weren't clean the germs would stick and spread, get mixed in other peoples' food. If there were germs in other people's food, they would get sick, and people's families would need to then take care of them. If people's families then needed to take care of them, they might spend all their money, trying just to keep them well. And if their families ran out of money, they might feel desperate and do things that feel wrong to make ends meet. The other people might then sleep all through the day, work through the night, stop eating, sleep instead of eat, or drink brown, bitter fluids, and/or they might take one shitty third shift job after another, sliding deep into some dark vat full of dirty blades.

*

He spirals down, down to another vat, down to the bottom of the blades. He shuffles back. He shines a light across the ground. Small clumps of ooze, strewn over black. Flat, wet, like dead fish, which he scrapes to sand, then rinses til the floor gleams like some steely arctic ocean.

He thinks of death.

He thinks of death.

The harness tugs.

He thinks of death.

He thinks, don't be a pussy.

He says, yeah, now.

Coming up.

As David climbs up from the vat, he feels tired, emptied out, like he's scraped off too much, left something he needs behind.

*

He snaps the blue gloves from his hands and tosses them. Runs warm water, scrubs his fingers, shakes them off, and dries.

He drives home through the dirty yellow-gray of morning. The sky is snowing clean white flakes into the muddy banks of ice.

He looks up at the mountains, tall and white. Up at the coal piles, tall and black and white. He rubs beneath his eyes with the sleeves of his shirt. His car climbs up the mountains, curves around, along them. To his left: the valleys and low slopes of towns, grey drifts of smoke, rising. To his right: the hills of bare-stripped birch, wreathed in a fringe of frosted pines. The car's old engine groans with effort. David's stomach growls.

He feels hungry, nauseous. He absorbs these little breaths of need, slight stirrings deep beneath a wave of numb, blurred chill.

He thinks, he likes the chill. He thinks, my father, brothers. They have also felt this chill. They know this feeling. They know what it means.

He sips black coffee from a plastic thermos, thinking about what it means. He doesn't know. He doesn't need to know. He looks down at the gray-white, teal houses from the mountain road. He thinks of all the brothers, fathers, living there inside them.

He thinks about the story that his father told so many times, about the leanest years, of how his mom would fry one egg for breakfast. Just a single egg, supposedly, that she would then set on a saucer plate they'd slide between them, back and forth, and back, and forth.

*

Morning upon morning upon morning. The tired plodding to the bedroom. Bag dropped on the floor. Shoe scuffle, slump of clothes shrugged off into a clumsy pile. Pulling back the drapes. Black curtains. Fall. The bed goes creak. Those ancient springs. A brief whiff of the weak, worn metal coils. Shudder. Creak. Creak. Crrreeeak. Something about that sound, that smell, means everything to him. Pull up the covers to his chin. Hands cold beneath. Cupped to his stomach. Pray for sleep. Please. Sleep. Please. Nothing, nothing, nothing. Please. Black curtains on his mind. Frayed edges. Block the light. Now, nothing, nothing, nothing, nothing, nothing, nothing, nothing, nothing, nothing, nothing, nothing, nothing, nothing, nothing............................ Now, there's a high-pitched something. Whining. Whining. Seeping. Through the curtains' edge. Light. Noise. Light, piercing. Please, shut up, shut up..Black curtains, curling into smoke, into the ether of his dreams, a shadow passing, fading, slipping into nothing, nothing, nothing, nothing, nothing...Now, another high-pitched cry. Olivia. Another high-pitched cry. Olivia, Olivia, he hears Emily whisper, hissing from behind the wall. The cries get softer. But, they do not stop, and now, the curtain of his sleep has slit wide open.

*

David was happy when Olivia was born a girl. He had some vague idea girls were easier to care for. He figured girls were quieter than boys, ate less, took up less space. He figured Emily, at least, was like that.

David was happy that Olivia looked more like Emily than him. He thought, of course that made sense, for a girl. At first, that made Olivia endear to him. Emily seemed content, having someone so close who so closely resembled her.

*

She's just like you, David's family keeps saying when they come to visit.

Thanks, Emily smiles, looking up and down.

They pass Olivia around the room. Emily watches them, glancing back and forth, scanning their movement anxiously.

I am so sorry, she says when Olivia begins to cry. She takes her daughter back into her arms and sighs.

She looks relieved. She looks content, like that.

She needs me, Emily remarks repeatedly to no one in particular.

*

The conversation hovers like a halo, no longer touching them. The two of them live like that, hovering in David's thoughts. Always a pair. Always absorbed in some strange language all their own. They may be there, in the room with him, but they're never really there.

*

The yellow undertones have faded from the gray sky when David pulls off on his exit, from the highway, into town. The snow is melting off the coal piles, and he sees the birch trees standing in their sparse formations, twig-thin, starving in the dust.

He sees the old sign for the Pine Burr Inn, open since 1962, although the windows now look dark. The unlit cursive neon and the daily special, all up-raised on long, white metal poles, seeming to rise above it all, just to announce that they still offer

Breakfast - Daily - 8am

Cold Beer TO GO

FRIDAY NIGHT KARAOKE

Scrapple & Eggs

Deuces X 2

He sees the homes with asphalt shingles, torn roofs on the outskirts of the town, the rust-red shit-creek with its patchy bits of half-disintegrated garbage. He drives along the main street, past the old dress factory, with its front paneling that bows—about to break—above the streets. He sees his parents' home, their old house, and the store where Emily works far less often than she used to. He drives past a block of mostly now abandoned buildings, watches a skeleton man and a woman poking their way through them.

He thinks about his town. He thinks about the buildings, thinks about the skeletons. They make him feel hungry. He thinks, I need to eat. He parks outside the main street diner that has come to be his favorite.

*

Emily realizes something is not right. Olivia cries all the time. She thinks the way she cries sounds strange.

David says, babies cry. That's what they do. They look around and they don't know what's going on. They don't know why they're crying.

Emily worries that Olivia is not eating enough. She cries for food, but never wants to eat.

David says she'll eat when she's hungry, which is true, though as the months go by, her skin looks pale, and she barely seems to grow.

Emily takes her to the doctor. She comes home with pamphlets filled with photographs of smiling children. Failure to thrive is what the doctor calls her food refusal. David thinks that this term makes Olivia sound like a plant.

Emily says that they should take her to the city to see specialists. They argue while Olivia sits, picking at the carpet fibers, rocking back and forth, humming. Hmmm-mm. Hmmm-mm. Hmmm-mm. David thinks that this noise makes Olivia sound like a robot.

He drives them to the city, trying hard to watch the road ahead despite his daughter's strange, distracting noises. Crrr-click. Crrr-click. Crrr-click. Crrr-click. Crrr-click, she hums, flicking her tongue against her teeth. David thinks that this noise makes Olivia sound like a bird.

*

He sits down in a paneled booth with dark green vinyl seats, a small, square, speckled table, and a vase of red carnations. There is a coffee cup already sitting on the table, on a saucer upside down. He turns it right side up.

A waitress comes and fills his coffee, asks what he will have. She knows he knows already: fried egg, toast, and bacon. She nods at him, then slides over to the only other customer, an old man in a trucker hat, another regular.

He taps a tab of creamer in his coffee. He watches as the milky tendrils sink in as he stirs. Some strands dive deep, dyeing the black a pale grayish brown. Some others catch inside the coffee's oil bubbled skin.

*

Olivia and Emily become a pair. They join a weekly meeting in the evenings. She has to rearrange her hours at her job, which means switching her shifts, or giving up shifts altogether.

Emily learns how to communicate with flashcards, image boards, and basic sign-language. This seems to help Olivia.

She's smart, Emily tells him. You just need to learn her signs. She's smart, she repeats, as though speaking of a stranger.

David tries to learn the signs the way she teaches him, but Emily keeps grabbing at his hands. She takes his fingers, bends them, waves them in different directions, saying, David, that's all wrong, that's not the way she does it.

*

The gray-lit shape she sees in bed, there, is not Emily, turned off onto her side, it is an outline shaped like Emily, filled in all wrong, slouched over in the wrong way, twisted up into the sheets all wrong, like someone who knew nothing, who knew neither of them, tried to make an Emily, Olivia stands, hand in mouth, looking at the not Emily, her stomach cold, knowing it will not move, it will not do the things that Emily would do, is not an Emily, but still, she moves toward the bed, knowing the room is wrong, the bed is wrong, the shape is wrong, the Emily is wrong, she moves the wrong way, hard cold in her stomach turning into liquid, moving through her arms, her legs, frozen and wrong, she leans all wrong, a not-Olivia, to look around the edges of the sheets, the opening, the edge of the not-Emily, the face hangs wrong, all colored wrong, all shaded wrong, green flowers, like the drawings of the ants that do not move, the not-Olivia cries, Emily, the not-Olivia looks down into the not-Emily's eyes, not open, not knowing, or thinking, open, not knowing why she cries, knowing that the flowers are not flowers, green, not leaves, not eyes, the not-Emily makes her angry, with her wrongness, with the wrongness of what made her like that, of what knows nothing about them, nothing about either of them, how the day is done, the springs creak, footsteps, door shuts, water runs, Emily standing in her nightgown, how the coffee makes the hungry-stomach sound, the not-Olivia's not stomach turns to boiling, everything all wrong, the hand inside her mouth, her hand, her not-mouth, all her not-inside-her, boiling, as she bites down, not quite feeling what her not-hand feels, everything her not-inside-her, not-insides, but biting harder, harder, harder, hard, until the boiling burns to vapor, and the vapor turns to cold, again, her stomach hardens, and her not-hand burns and bleeds...

*

Olivia grows taller, up to Emily's chest, shoulders, chin, as David measures, pencils marks into the wall. Each little scritch, scritch, scritch becomes a line of dashes, dates. He paints them over, that summer. Decides she isn't growing anymore.

Walking beside her, through the side streets to the store, or to the school, or the center where they have their weekly meetings, Emily notices the buildings seem much older than they did only— what feels like—a few short years ago. The clapboard houses smudged with streaks. Pale birchwood. Faded mauve. Black spots of mud, or mold, or coal. Torn strips like chewed up skin. Raw, soggy patches of the houses, peeling in puddles, running into sidewalks filled with cracks like crooked teeth.

They pass the white house with its wounded second floor, which is a rift of rotted wood where all the paneling was torn away. Frayed strands of insulation drape around the boarded windows. Emily clasps her hand tight around Olivia's blue glove.

*

They pass the mural of the town. The paint has long since flecked away. What's left is just some foggy seafoam outlines. If you didn't know to look, you wouldn't even see it.

Emily points, what is that, Olivia?

Olivia signs, blue, blue, blue.

*

Sometimes, less often now, they go to David's parents' house. Their family files through the kitchen while Olivia sifts through the tray of food she brought from home: rice crackers, carrot sticks, cucumbers sliced into small jagged circles.

Emily opens up the bag of things brought for Olivia, passing her fork, her cup, the sauce she likes to use. She takes Olivia's blue gloves and goes to clean them off. She waits for David's mother, who is filling up her water glass.

Her mother-in-law tilts the faucet toward Emily.

Thanks, Emily smiles as his mother makes that look she always makes, a mix of curiosity and sympathy, annoyance, and discomfort.

Do you have the...

Yes, her mother-in-law opens up a drawer. The special soap you like.

Emily nods. It's just...she puts these things inside her mouth.

She runs the water and her mother-in-law sighs.

That look, again, but with the sympathy dialed up, the curiosity dialed down.

She says, I don't know how you do it. I could never do it.

And before Emily can ask just what she means by it, before she can explain she doesn't really have a choice, her mother-in-law's look of curiosity becomes a look of plain discomfort.

It does seem you spoil her, a bit.

*

The living room wall photo albums have expanded. Now, there is a wall devoted just to grandkids (and to future grandkids). School photos—David's brother's little boy—starting with kindergarten, ending with this year, in the 5th grade. Olivia's small patch of wall begins and ends with baby pictures, even though she's almost 17, and she is beautiful, isn't she, with her mother's eyes, her hair, her nose, her mouth, her voice, her posture, and her mannerisms, yes...I see it...do you see it?

*

They're trying to be kind, of course. In town, the other mother and the other girl who move away as they walk by. She sees the mother squeeze the daughter's hand and hiss, watch where you're going, like she's teaching all of them a lesson.

Emily gets caught up, imagining the fine points of this lesson, and she stumbles, scrapes her heel on a sidewalk crack.

Olivia laughs, like she always does at clumsiness.

Emily mumbles, shit. The heel of her shoe is peeling off.

Emily takes Olivia inside the store where she works, sometimes, not from any strong affection for the space, but just because it's close. It has the things they need, like toilet paper, cigarettes, and

Ibuprofen, and she knows exactly where to find them. Even so, there are thin aisles—and Olivia takes time to walk through all of them, touching the head of each face on each box of Clairol hair dye—there are things like toys and makeup brushes—which Olivia must touch, must feel smooth strands, rough bristles, squishy rubber coils—there are buzzing lights—Olivia squints, presses both her hands against her ears, and hums—and there are people that she has worked with for years, who still say things like, how old is Olivia? How does she make that sound? Do you think she's okay? What do you think she could be thinking?

*

And then, of course, sometimes she doesn't feel like dealing with the same people she sees whenever she comes into work. But it's the same people, wherever they decide to go, among the small amount of choices they have in this town.

And it's the same strangeness, wherever they decide to go. Attempting to extract her tendrilled fingers from a vine of grapes. Attempting to explain the brillo pad is not a brush, and even if it were a brush, we do not use it in the store. Attempting to conceal her small delight when things get knocked over, or pushed aside, and part of Emily can't help but feel, fuck these people, fuck these things, and who the fuck am I, to say don't look at that, don't do that, don't touch that, don't feel that way.

An old man, hunching over, in a walk that looks impossible.

A frail young man, wandering, scratching at his pock marks.

A woman who stands, yelling at nobody in particular, I need some service! Can I get some service over here?

The cashier lady with the froth of hair who's always saying things like, that's the Lord's way, and they're all God's children, aren't they?

The police officer, one bad day, who suggests, politely, she does not have full control of this: the situation.

*

Olivia follows the line of light to the door, does not look back until she closes it behind her with a click.

But she looks at the door.

She listens to the branches, scratching.

Water, tapping.

In the pipes.

Behind the wall.

Behind the door.

*

Olivia follows the grooves of the living room floor, which form a scratchy circle she has always thought of as a nest.

Her bare feet scrape along the branches of the nest, circling, scraping, all around the opening that isn't really there.

She paces, scraping.

Humming.

Puts her hand inside her mouth and hums into her fingers and her wet skin, all the cold warmth underneath.

The window box, wrapped up in plastic for the winter, breathes in crinkled breaths, as air fills up the spaces in between.

The air folds

    in

        and out

           in soft waves...

              in

         and out

     crr-creak...   and in

      crr-creak...   and out   and in

   crr-creak...   and out

and in   crr-creak...

 and out   and out

    crr-creak...   and in

     crr-creak...   and out

          and in

*

The air gets louder as the gravel pops and cracks, as they drive higher up away from town along the mountain road. Tonight, the moon is just a sliver, like the way the road looks from the town. Emily thinks, that's where we live. The moon.

The radio is playing, softly, statically, but no one is really listening until Olivia picks up some resonance she likes. She hums a pleasant accidental harmony, and David laughs. Emily laughs. Olivia laughs at their laughing.

It is a late fall night. The smell of burning leaves has been replaced by smells of burnt ash buried underneath the frost. The cold damp of the wind picks up the coal dust. David thinks, it is a lonely smell, the coal dust blowing in the cold. He thinks about the old coal fireplace his parents used to use. It was a pain to load, to clean, and honestly, it smelled bad. But he feels strange now, standing in his own front yard, with his own family, looking down at the town, breathing the lonely cold.

*

But Olivia loves the quiet and the lonely cold. She loves the bowl of small lights down below. She loves the long tree shadows all around the house. She loves the way the dark spreads out its fingers over everything. She loves stretching to touch the edges of her room. She loves to see things with her fingers, loves to tell it all goodnight.

Goodnight, town.

Goodnight, cold hill.

Goodnight, nest floor.

Goodnight, white walls.

Goodnight, bird calls.

Goodnight, branches.

Goodnight, wind.

*

Goodnight, stars.

Goodnight, sky.

Goodnight, ice voices in the pipes.

She hears them whispering:

Good-bye,

good-bye,

good-bye,

good-bye,

good-bye.

*

David spends more time with his parents, now—his family. Emily and Olivia begin to feel like his other family: a family of feelings, language, future preparations that do not belong to him, are not his own.

He knows that Emily is worried about where Olivia will go. She spends her days off on the phone with social service leaflets spread around her on the table, going over options. She keeps a notebook with her at all times, jotting things down, biting the insides of her mouth, nodding, mhm, mhm. When she gets up to take a break, David glances down at the notebook. It is mostly filled with acronyms like ODP, ABA, DDC, and euphemistic phrases like empower, advocate, discovery, transitions.

Meanwhile, Olivia sits humming softly in the living room, watching the Weather Channel with her gloved hand in her mouth. He coughs, and she looks up at him, closes her mouth, and gently puts the gloved hand in her lap.

*

When David's mother opens her front door, the whole house smells like dinner rolls and melted butter, fresh and warm and wonderful.

His mother pats his back. You hungry? Like she has to ask.

He cracks a beer. So hungry I could fucking die.

He loads his plate with all his favorite foods since he was five. Going back to his parents' feels like being five years old, with beer. Scalloped potatoes that melt in your mouth, potato salad, and pierogis. Anyone who says that's too many potatoes can fuck off. He sinks deep down into that ancient, shapeless marvel of a couch next to his brother, who is yelling out his brains, like always. Drinks his beer. His mother brings another, and another.

He fake protests—like he always does. No, Ma, I have to drive back home.

His mother nudges him. This is your home. And don't forget that.

And it doesn't sound—or feel—like she's joking.

*

Emily is in bed with another headache—which is bound to happen, David guesses, when you spend your life absorbed in things that cause them. She's been having them more often, but she's getting older, and Olivia's a constant, humming hover-cloud.

He sits next to Olivia. She turns and looks at him, unreadably, then turns and looks back to the Weather Channel. They sit and watch the Weather Channel, which is really quite relaxing with its peaceful music, maps, and simple diagrams. The icons of the sun, the cloud, the rain—they look a little like the flashcards and the schedule that she uses, David notices.

You like the Weather Channel? He smiles as Olivia keeps humming, glancing from the screen, down to her hand.

He gets her soup for lunch. He pours the can into the pot. Olivia walks over to the stove, making a sound almost like cooing. She leans over, slightly, carefully, to see the bubbles pop. A really big one pops. She makes a little squeak.

You want to stir the pot? He offers, and she takes the spoon and stirs. She scrapes the spoon against the inside of the pot, he sees. She seems to understand. He gets so caught up watching her that he almost forgets to say, Olivia, turn off the stove.

Later that afternoon, he works with her on Words, using her flashcards and a dry-erase board with a blue blueberry-scented marker. He says, write your name—he points between the dashed grid of the guiding lines—O-L-I-V-I-A, that spells Olivia. She writes the O, a sharp line for the L, then makes a light _, then a tiny v, a swift I, then she pauses at the A. She makes a ^ with both her index fingers, taps her fingertips together, draws a ^ shape on the board, then draws the —.

Olivia! Good job! High five! She smiles as he raises his flat hand, flattens out her own hand, gives him a quick, timid tap.

Hey Em! She wrote her name! He calls out to the bedroom.

Emily calls back, she's known her name for years, you idiot.

*

He listens to the humming of fluorescent lights inside the plant. He used to hate that sound, but now it makes him sad. It's not like drones, or bugs—or whatever he thought—but hidden instruments that play one note, that never finish getting started.

He sprays the walls, the floors, the stainless steel machines with blasts of pressurized soap spray: a thick, whitewash of foam. He watches as the mist clears, soap strands dripping, draining down in streams. The bubbles pop. He thinks, Olivia would love this.

hmmmmmmmmmmmmmmmmmmmmmm
mmmmmmmmmmmmmmmmmmmmmmmm
mmmmmmmmmmmmmmmmmmmmmmmmm
mmmmmmmmmmmmmmmmmmmmmmmmmm
mmmmmmmmmmmmmmmmmmmmmmmmmmm
mmmmmmmmmmmmmmmmmmmmmmmmmm
mmmmmmmmmmmmmmmmmmmmmm
mmmmmmmmmmmmmmmmmmmmmmmmmmm
mmmmmmmmmmmmmmmmmmmmmmmmmmmmmmmmmm
mmmmmmmmmmmmmmmmmmmmmmmmmmmmmmm
mmmmmmmmmmmmmmmmmmmmm
mmmmmmmmmmmmmmmmmmm   mmmmmmmmmmmm
mmmmmmmmmmmmm   mmmmmmmmmmmmmmm
mmmmmmmmmmmmmmmmmmmmmmmmmmmmmmmm
mmmmm   mmmmmmmmmm   good-bye,
mmmmm
mmmmmmmmmmmmmmm   mmmmmmmmmmmmmmmm
mmmmmmmmmmm good-bye,   mmmmmmmmmmmmmmmmm
mmmmmmmmmm   mmmmmmmmmmmm
mmmmmmm   mmmmmmmmmmm
mmmmmmmmmmmmmmmm
Good-bye, good-bye, good-bye
hmmmmmmmmmmm   mmmmmmmm

mmm   mmmm

mmm   mm   mmm

,,,,,,,

,,,,

in

and out

72

and in

and mmmmmmmmm

mmmm   mmmm

mmmm

,,,,,,,,

,,,,

,,,,

,,,   ,,

,,,,,

and out

and in

and out

and in

,,

,,

,,,,

,,,   ,,

,,,,,

,,,,

,,,   ,,

,,,,,

Goodbye, goodbye, goodbye

Goodbye,

goodbye,,,

goodbye,,,,

,,,

,,

,,

,

Olivia now circles.
As the sky now changes.
Crinkled breath slows.
And the slivers spread.
The gray light bleeds.
The floor-nest-branch.
Now breaks.
Her bare skin.
Breaks.
She jumps.
She cries.
Her cry rings.
Shaking.
Hovering.
A high-pitched.
Humming.
Through the walls.

*

She pads into the kitchen, stops, and looks down at her foot.

The pain is fluttering inside her skin, like needle wings.

She stands, now, looking out the picture window where Emily would be, should be, there, in her blue nightgown with white stripes.

The branches are bare brown. There is no sun or sunshine. The sky is gray-blue, Emily's gray-blue. It is the flashcard color she would be.

Olivia pictures a white rectangle, and a square patch of the sky with Emily beneath.

*

Emily sits on the edge of the bed, leaning, hands pressed into her knees. Her head feels fluttery. Her chest hurts, like her heart is rolling loose, bumping and bruising things. She mumbles, mm. She folds her head between her knees and hums, mmmmmmmmmmm.

She closes her eyes. She pictures her heart as a boulder, rolling to the edge of some familiar cliff, like Lover's Leap. She breathes in, out, and in, imagining the boulder, rolling back into the mountain, rolling itself back in place. Her head begins to clear. She fluffs the pillow on her side, pulls up the sheets. Smoothes over David's empty side. His sheets are cold. The bed springs go crr-creak as she shifts over them. She hears Olivia's crr-creak immediately follow hers.

*

Sometime around 12:30, when she's scraping dishes and Olivia is wiping down the table, as she always does, Emily hears David's springs go crrrrr-crrr-creak, and she hears him yawn and stand.

She goes to ask if he would like some breakfast/lunch/dinner.

She opens the door while he's changing, pulling up his underwear. He looks strange there, with his hair mussed, half undressed. She likes his hair, though, how it curls a little wild, how it's thinned in patches where the silver tangles shine. She likes his body, his strong neck, his broad shoulders, his chest, his muscles grooved in hair that's also curled, but dark. She even likes his stomach, looming roundly, heavily, the skin still firm, still taut, above the shadow of his cock. His cock is hanging awkward and balloonish, grayish-pinkish. Like a cartoon nose she thinks. A sick cartoon nose! And she giggles.

David looks up, squints. What are you laughing at?

She swallows. Sorry...I don't think...I don't know.

He looks down, where her eyes are looking.

She looks down, embarrassed, at the floor.

*

David rolls over, stiffly—maybe still asleep—in bed. He leans into Emily's shoulder, fingers searching, kissing clumps of hair. His beard hair muffles low groans as he reaches for her nightgown. Fingers soft and fumbling. She sighs. He is asleep.

She shifts away from him. He mumble-growls something that isn't words, and she says, firmly, back to bed. It's late. The firmness of her voice sounds wrong, she realizes, like she's reprimanding, like she's talking to Olivia.

He grips around her shoulder, pulls her back toward him, forcefully, mumbling more not-words.

She says, no, David!

He exhales sharply in a long hiss, seems to come-to in the dark. He whispers, Emily?

She pulls her nightgown down. Go back to sleep.

Was I asleep? He says.

You did that thing again, she says. That sleep sex thing.

Oh, shit. He says, I didn't mean...I'm sorry.

It's okay, she says in a flat voice, feeling strange about her accidental slip into the voice she uses with Olivia. She thinks about how she thought, sick cartoon nose, and this makes her so sad that she wants to touch him, wants to bury all her wrong thoughts and wrong voices in his warmth, but it is late, and she is tired, and he is already sleeping when she leans over to kiss him.

He wants me in his sleep, at least, she thinks. She squints into the dark, imagining the vague, gray shapes into another room inside another town, another time, where they can both meet in their sleep, and come together, be together, just the two of them.

*

Meanwhile, Emily's mother is up there, on the sixth floor of the high-rise, sleeping in a thin bed with a thin sheet and a metal rail. But she is not there, not in her dreams, in the thin room, or the thin bed, or the thin, sick body that is lying in it. She is walking through the town, not in the seafoam fog, the black smudged clapboard, broken sidewalks, windows, and abandoned buildings. She is walking as a young girl, past the barbershop, the mural, and the drugstore with its clean tile and chrome lettering. She walks into the blonde brick movie theater, buys a ticket for the matinee. She shuffles down the aisle, which is lit with paneled strips that run along the walls, small greenish sconces, and a grand globe ceiling lamp in ornate painted moulding. She sits down in the middle row, eases herself into the velveteen red cushion, careful not to squeak the hinges. She feels quiet hovering above her like a strange perfume, and all around her, there are men and women, sitting similarly, breathing in the same sourceless perfume. Their ears are trained. Their eyes are focused on the still-closed curtains. There's a hum of expectation growing up around the unseen screen. Soon to fall. Soon to glow. All hushed and waiting for the lights to dim.

*

Gray-blue.

Bare brown.

No sun or sunshine.

Something falling that is neither rain, nor snow.

A sound that's something lighter than a tapping.

The whisper-crackle of the wind around the plastic-covered unit.

In and out and in and out and in. She breathes. Her hand stings.

She looks back from the window. Pads across the floor.

Some grit sticks to her bare feet. Coffee grounds.

She looks down, looks up at the bright green.

Dashes—they are numbers—on the stove clock.

The bright green number dashes now say 7:30.

*

Emily says good morning gray-blue cloudy sky a chance of showers snow the time is 7:30 now the clock says 7:30 what do we do now first let me help you remember what do we do now let me help you remember Olivia look at your chart Olivia the clock says 7:30 chart says Up at 7:30 on the clock the chart the sky is gray-blue morning 7:30 on the green clock 7:30 on the green leaf card the clock the chart the sky the chance of rain or partial sunshine 7:30 so good morning 7:30 so the clock the chart the card the cloud they say Get Up Get Up Get Up Olivia.

*

It is raining the morning they go to visit the group home for adults with special needs, as Emily now calls Olivia. She feels forced to use these words, which do not seem to fit, although Olivia has special needs and she is technically adult. She doesn't look adult while tip-toe sloshing to the car in rain boots, doesn't sound adult while humming softly with the radio, and Emily has come to feel most of her needs are not that special; they're just ordinary things she can't communicate.

But she hums happily because she likes the car. She likes the rain. Emily watches in the rearview as Olivia traces her fingers from the window top, down to the bottom, following the pathway of the drops.

They leave Olivia at David's mother's house, which Emily hates doing, hates how she refers to herself as The Grandma. It is always The Grandma, not Olivia's Grandma, not that Olivia would call her Grandma, if she ever thought of her that way. She hates that dumb wall, those dumb photos, the dumb way his mother acts confused when she shows her the items in Olivia's big bag—of food, activities, spare clothes, and other ordinary items—which she feels compelled to call The Special Bag. David dislikes The Bag, the way it makes his mother so confused, the way he knows she will not use most of those items anyway, the way Emily always gets upset when they pick up Olivia and she sees things unopened and uneaten.

Hello, Granddaughter, his mother coos.

Olivia is blank-faced.

Are those presents for me? She jokes when they hand her The Special Bag.

Enjoy your visit! She calls, waving from the door as though they're driving off to see an old friend, someone they both know.

*

The car feels quiet even with the radio turned on. The drive feels long. It is long, taking them out to the middle of some nowhere. Past shit-creek, a dark rush of orange in the rain. Past houses with their asphalt siding, peeling to reveal their inner ooze.

A penny for your thoughts, he breaks the silence without looking at her.

That much? She says.

Don't be dumb, he says. What's going on in there?

She sighs. I don't know, David, watching as a thin, pale girl appears to eat a blade of grass she picks from her front lawn.

I just can't know what you don't tell me, Em, he says.

She says, I know, but...

She looks back. The girl is still there, on the muddy lawn. Still eating grass.

I think whatever choice we make will suck. David, our options suck.

He shrugs, well, okay then. Nice talking to you, Emily.

*

They drive down, past the bottom of the hill where everything just stops, just flattens out to ranch homes, big lawns, farms. They drive on, passing bigger farms and old, white houses, horse-drawn carriages. They look so small against the mountains in the background. They pull up a thin road, up to an ordinary-looking ranch home with a metal ramp along the side for wheelchairs. They ring the doorbell, and Emily hears a shuffling inside, a few weird whining cries, a set of squeaking footsteps.

A big-shouldered man with a buzzed haircut opens the door. You must be Emily and David.

Emily nods.

David says, hi.

Olivia's parents, right?

Emily nods again.

All right. I'll try to show you what it's like around here.

He leads them to the living room, a fairly ordinary-looking room with bare walls, slightly sunk-in couches. Two young men sit, watching TV. One man is doing laundry, stacking it inside the hamper, fumbling to fold a dishrag. The other man is rocking back and forth, clapping his hands, getting excited by the show they're watching: COPS.

Bad boys, bad boys! He sings.

David notices the TV is a flatscreen.

Emily notices the TV is encased in plastic, points. What's up with that?

Big-shouldered man shrugs. Sometimes, JB gets worked up, and when he does, he looks for things to smash.

The kitchen is an ordinary kitchen. Clean. A little bare. No knives out. A man stands over the stove, cooking something with boiled cabbage.

Haluski, he says, smiling.

David thinks, it smells good.

Emily thinks, Olivia would not eat that.

There are two bathrooms, says their guide. Both have a walk-in shower. Here's the main one that we use. It is an ordinary-looking bathroom with the slight exception of a laundry chute, duct-taped and zip-tied in a strange configuration.

What's that? Says Emily.

Let's just say sometimes, things go down the laundry chute that weren't ever meant to go down there, says their guide.

This place is big, thinks David. Wish we had two bathrooms.

Emily thinks of all the things that could go down a laundry chute.

They walk together down the long hall with the bedrooms: six in all. A thin and boyish man paces, his shoe soles scraping, squeak, squeak, squeak. He wears a tight-knit lycra shirt stretched over his whole torso. Both sleeves flop loose, both his arms pinned tight against him. Their tour is interrupted by a sudden wail, rushing footsteps, and the sounding of a high-pitched door alarm.

Shit, sorry, says their guide. JB's a maniac.

Emily looks at David.

David sighs.

*

David goes to the living area to see if help is needed. Emily continues walking down the hall. There is a girl who lives here. They said on the phone. A quiet girl. They said Olivia could have the room across from her's.

Emily finds the quiet girl down at the hall's end, in the farthest room, propped up inside a metal hospital bed. Her head is turned toward the door, although Emily notices her eyes do not shift when a stranger enters her room.

The girl's bed sheets are damp.

The room smells wet, like stale urine.

She is wearing a blue bib around her neck.

It's wet as well.

Her mouth is open.

She is breathing in soft gurgles.

She is making little rhythmic, clicking noises, like a turn signal.

There is a chart above her bed for staff to initial for checks. Just like the bathroom door, at work, Emily thinks.

She checks the chart. According to the chart, it's been four hours.

Four whole fucking hours, Emily thinks, since they've looked at you.

*

It's not that bad, says David.

Silence.

What? Says David.

More silence.

It is a nice house. Bigger than ours. Nicer than ours, really, David says.

More silence.

And more silence.

And more silence.

And more silence.

Fuck you, David says. He switches on the radio.

*

There is the world as it is—as it has always been—for Emily. The world of the town, the mural of the town. The world of chipped paint, boarded windows, beautiful things, ugly things, of two extremes, always together, blending into one. The world of paper rotted into walls, of walls bending and bowing, wires tangled into vines, the shit-creek, of all things that people lose, or toss, forget about, inside that creek, turning in small, frustrated circles, burning, and disintegrating, into nothing. The world of such small things, of small changes, of constant changes, in a world so full of them, too many to make note of, notice, of small deaths, small near deaths, small illnesses, and small losses that all felt like no big deal, felt like nothing, felt like life.

*

There is the world for Olivia. The world of 7:30, 7:45, 8:15, 8:30, 8:35, 8:45, 9:00, 10:00, 11:00, 11:30, 12:00, 12:30, 1:00, 1:30, 2:00. The world of Up, Eat, Clean, Med, Brush Teeth, Dress, Play, Words, Eat, Clean, Med, Brush Teeth, Bed. The world of flashcards, shuffled, stacked, one drawn after another, one thing after another, of frequent interruptions like the crinkle, crinkle, tap, tap, scratch, cooroo, coo coo, cooroo, coo coo, coroo, coo coo. The world where small sounds and small sensations feel so big, so beautiful, so full of strangeness, like at any moment, anything could change, change into something even bigger, even louder, even stranger, like at any moment, anything could happen.

*

There is a word for David's world. It is Family. It is—as it has always been—a word for comfort, closeness, for the walls covered in images of Family, the walls all warm, the smells of butter, bread, cheese, and potatoes, stove sweat, warm, wet air, smells coming from the kitchen, beer, TV, forever-flowing through the living room, a current ever-flowing through the house, the soft couch, Family sunk-in, down, next to you, watching the TV, watching the same thing, cheering for the same thing, hoping for the same thing, for the life they have—that they have always had, together—as a Family, of comfort, closeness, images all warm, the TV, glowing, butter, bread, forever-flowing from the kitchen, to the living room, all through the house, the home, of what he knows as Family.

*

We are a family—I know—we are your family—I know—we have our own home, we have worked hard for—I know, I know—we have a place—I know—there is a place to put Olivia, a nice place—honestly—oh, honestly, what did you think it would be like—the morning forecast—not a nice place, David—fuck—a nice place—listen—no—with scattered clouds—that girl, that girl, they put her in the back room—oh my God, enough already with that girl, that girl, of course they put her in the back room, yeah, maybe it's not the best place ever, but it's what they have to work with—chance of rain—that boy, they pay attention to that noise—Jesus, Emily, what should they do then, just let them run into the street—of slight wind—that is not the point—the point, the point is that we have a place where she can go—Olivia—Olivia can go, and she'll be fine, there—she'll be fine—she will, and you—of morning fog, then sunshine—she will not be fine—no, YOU will not be fine, is what you mean—oh is that what I mean, please tell me—scattered showers—Jesus—I can't, David, I can't live with myself, knowing every day, that she is there, that she

90

is, I can't live, not knowing how she feels—you don't know now, how she feels—maybe not, but—scattered showers—no, you'll never know that, Em, you'll never know, and I will never know—a chance of rain—and so, I should just let her go, just put her in some shit hole—it is not a fucking shit hole—it is, David, it's a fucking shit hole—rain, throughout—Emily—I can't, I can't—I, I, I, you, you, you, it's all about you, isn't it—no—it is all about you isn't it—a shit hole—no, shut up, no, it always was you, you know, you have always felt this way, you, you, you, always you, you, you, you fucking head-case—shh—I'm right—shh, shh—oh shh, shh, shh yourself—a mild morning, light cloud-cover, picking up mid-afternoon with gusts of 20 mile-per-hour wind and scattered showers for the rest of the day, so dress for the weather, don't forget to bring your—

*

Emily switches off the TV, and as if on cue, Olivia cries out, a siren-like wail, with no tears, no sniffling, no sadness in her eyes, that they can see, no readable expression, just a wideness, just a strangeness, just a wail. Then, she pauses for a breath, sucks in some air, makes an expression so unreadable it's funny, and Emily laughs a weird and breathy laugh. Olivia begins to wail again, now even louder, and Emily laughs, and laughs, and laughs, and laughs, and laughs, and laughs.

*

The bright green number dashes now say 7:30, so she thinks, get
Up, get Up, and go look at your schedule. It says:

7:30 am - 7:45 am	Up
7:45 am - 8:15 am	Eat
8:15 am - 8:30 am	Clean
8:30 am - 8:35 am	Med
8:35 am - 8:45 am	Brush teeth
8:45 am - 9:00 am	Dress
9:00 am - 10:00 am	Play
10:00 am - 11:00 am	Words
11:00 am -11:30 am	TV
11:30 am - 12:00 pm	Cook
12:00 pm - 12:30 pm	Eat
12:30 pm - 1:00 pm	Clean

She is already Up. She walks across the kitchen floor until the
bright green number dashes fall into the right place.

She takes one step. Looks down.

Cold white-gray floor, flecked. Scrawls of light.

Two steps. Looks up.

The bright green number dashes now say 7:31.

One step. Looks down.

The scrawls of light sway. Soft, skeletal waves.

Two steps. Looks up.

The bright green number dashes now say 7:32.

She puts her hand inside her mouth. It's cracked, still bleeding. Tastes like blood. Her teeth trace torn skin, tonguing lightly, as the scrawls of light sway, fluttering.

Now 7:33.

Now 7:34.

Now 7:35.

7:40.

7:45.

It is time to eat, and she is very hungry. She plods to the pantry, gets the cereal, and sets it on the table. She walks up to the cabinet. One step, looks down. Two steps, looks up. She gets the small bowl from the low shelf, sets it on the counter. Slides the drawer open. Shh, shh. It sounds the way it always does. She gets the spoon. She sets the spoon and bowl down on the table. She walks up to the fridge. One step, looks down. Two steps, looks up. Opens the door and stands in cold light. Smells like old milk.

She takes the carton to the table, sets it down, sucks in a breath, gathering something in her head and in her stomach all together. Looks toward Emily's door. Looks down. Looks up. Looks back at the arrangement of the items on the table.

She scoops 1, 2, 3, 4 scoops of the cereal into the bowl. This is the part where Emily would usually pour the milk. She holds the milk in both hands, estimating. Opens it, and smells. Pinches her nose. Puts it back down. Puts it away.

She pulls the chair out. It squeaks loud across the floor. Cc-creak. She hisses breath. Sss, ss. She sits down. Takes a bite of milkless cereal. Crr-crunch.

She looks down at the drawn ants on the tablecloth, not real ants. She counts, one ant. She takes another bite. She counts, two ants...

*

Emily says, wake up. Or David says, wake up. Maybe nobody says it. Either way, neither of them seems much obliged to be awake for whatever it is they're doing. Rubbing up against each other. Dipping sort of in, but mostly out, and out, and out, of one another. It seems hardly real. How her arm moves through this numb fuzz. How her recognition of each movement comes so far after the fact. The way she feels like her own echo. The coal fog, stale milk sex smell somehow just seems to pull out from the walls. Her stuck together eyelids. Sour drizzled brillo-beard. How everything feels nightmare-heavy, like some ghost you try to run away from, just to find your legs are liquid. They are liquid, so lead-heavy, so paint-poisonous. So so, so so. So on. The smell of semen, coal. The sound of morning birds, and wind, and of a soft cock, tapping cold and wet against her thigh.

95

*

David feels hungry, nauseous. He tries to absorb these little breaths of need, slight stirrings deep beneath a wave of dumb, blurred chill. But sometimes, he just can't absorb them, and he drives homeward, into the dark, knowing he now needs something more to try to numb them.

He passes by the Pine Burr Inn, the still-dark rooms, the old sign with the unlit cursive neon and the daily special which now reads

> Breakfast - Daily - 8am
> Cold Beer TO GO
> FRIDAY NIGHT KARAOKE
> CLOSED SUNDAY
> beef bur undy sup
> french to

He pulls up to a bar just outside of town, a white-gray clapboard house that looks like it could be somebody's home. He sits down in a paneled booth with dark green vinyl seats. He sips a cold green bottled beer, and then another one. The cigarette smoke hangs thick in the air, thick in the pale foam insulation spilling out from cracks inside the vinyl. A tingling sensation gathers in his throat, moves through his chest. He peels the label on his bottle, makes a small pile with the shreds.

The few remaining people are already drunk, or drunk enough, or steady-buzzed enough to go about their day, except for one small woman reaching in her wallet, counting, quiveringly, out-loud, 36, 37, 43 cents. Her voice sounds childish, counting like that. She is young, he realizes, really not much older than Olivia. He thinks about Olivia, what she'll be doing when she's 21. He thinks, not much. There isn't much here to be done.

David puts a dollar on the bar for her. The woman looks up, and her face is somehow simultaneously worn—shadowed and puffed—and startlingly quite attractive. She takes her beer and smiles with half-embarrassed half-relief.

She says, thank you for your help, and she sounds like she means it.

She holds her bottle up.

He clinks his own against it.

She sips and sighs like it's the best thing she has ever tasted.

David sips and nods and thinks, maybe it is.

*

This is the part where Emily should put her coffee cup down, look up, and say, time to help clean up, Olivia. This is the part where Olivia should pick up her bowl and spoon and take it to the sink and run clean water over it to rinse the crumbs. This is the part where she should hear Emily's springs go creak, a yawn, a set of footsteps. This is the part where Emily should open up her bedroom door. This is the part where Olivia should see her, standing there, at the window, in a blue nightgown with thin white stripes.

Olivia picks up her bowl and spoon and takes them to the sink. She sets the bowl down on the metal bottom of the sink, fills it with water, dumps the water down the drain, and listens to the water cllggh-ccll, like the hungry-stomach-sound of coffee being made. She turns the spoon under the tap, rinsing the round side, turns it over, and gets splashed. She makes a loud sound of surprise. The sound fills up the house, echoing, almost like two voices, and Olivia keeps turning back and looking at the bedroom door.

The clock says 8:15. It's time for Emily to say, two pumps of soap, to wet the wash rag so Olivia can wipe the waxy table cloth, so she can count 24 ants, so she can drape the wet cloth down around the faucet like a scarf.

Olivia counts, two pumps. Wipes the table down, watches the way it shines, the way it always shines, and feels wrong. The cereal scratches hard like dry claws inside her stomach, as she hears the birds.

Cooroo

coo coo

Cooroo

coo coo

Cooroo

coo coo

*

The sky is always like the ocean. It is always there, but never really there, never a depth that she can swim to, sink into. Emily pictures sinking into all of life's impossibilities, the cold, the dark, of all she does not know. It is a winter night. She's tired, but she can't sleep, and she can't stop thinking of the distance from the closet to the bedroom door, the distance from the bedroom door out to the front door, and the distance from the front door to the car. She pictures gray light, salted snowdrifts, all the names of states she'd pass: Ohio, Indiana, Illinois, Missouri, Oklahoma—or Nebraska—Colorado—Texas—Utah—or New Mexico—Nevada—Arizona, California. She imagines all the light just getting warmer, brighter, rosier, the mountains yawned in mauve haze like some soft, forever-sunset, which just ends in ocean, ends in depths she cannot picture, though she tries to picture them, she sees flat colors on a map, the drawing of an ocean—real water does not look like that—is not so bright, is not so wide, so blue—no, real water is a puddle, or an orange creek, a coldness underneath—which she feels rifting, rushing—pulling her back, all across the map, through Arizona—or Nevada—Utah—or New Mexico—Texas—or Colorado—Oklahoma—or Nebraska, through Missouri, Illinois, Indiana, Ohio, through the salt snow, back through coal-dark patches, threads of birch, and houses leaning in the hills, back to their small gray house, her own house, her own home.

*

When David tells her he is leaving, she is not surprised. Why would she be? He's simply going down the hills, back to his real home. It's almost funny, how he talks about the distance, like he's moving from some foreign country, re-learning his local language.

You mean the bar, says Emily.

I mean, things have been hard for years, he says.

She nods. You sound like them, the people in the bar.

It's just been hard, Em. Things just aren't supposed to be this hard.

She looks at him and laughs at this idea.

It's funny how he keeps saying he cares about them, how she knows he does—probably does—but he is just too dumb to understand what he is really saying when he says, over and over, they will be fine, they're all going to be fine.

*

They are all fine. The door shuts and the sound rings through the house, and every sound that follows feels like a kind of cover-up.

The automated systems.

Make a payment.

No.

More information.

No.

Repeat the menu.

No.

Speak to a representative.

They quickly form their rhythm, Emily and Olivia. They were—they are—after all, better off here as a pair. Emily hangs the schedule on the wall. She throws away the blue gloves. Goes through closets, tosses clothes in bags, including her work shirt. Feels lighter. Emptier, from time to time. Lightheaded. Watching the clock as one green digit flickers into the next.

*

They are all fine.

They are all fine.

They had to be the way they are.

They are a sad story, of course, that David tells when he has had enough to drink, when someone asks about his family, and he knows he's supposed to know which family they mean. And they are fine. And they fit in now, into their respective spaces.

Where they want to be.

Their own home.

His own home.

With all the buttered rolls that he could ever eat.

With no disruptions to his sleep.

With no disruptions to his schedule, now made only of what he does not do, like:

7:30 am	No, too early for a drink.
8:30 am	No, too early for a drink.
9:00 am	No, too early for a drink.
10:00 am	No, too early for a drink.

*

This is how the morning now begins: she hears the birds, cooroo coo coo, gets up, looks at her schedule, goes into the kitchen. She stands with her elbows propped against the counter as she waits for the green digits to say 7:30. She takes the bowl and spoon out from the cabinet. Scoops cereal into her bowl, and eats crr crunch crr crunch, and takes the bowl back to the sink. Rinses the bowl and spoon. Wipes off the table. Brushes her teeth. Gets dressed in her blue shirt with white polka dots, her gray pants, and her white socks with blue ridges. Sits and looks at all her flashcards. Brown dog, brown dirt. Yellow lemon, yellow sun. Blue water, blue fish. Green frog, green leaf. Gray mouse, gray mountain. Pictures a card with a gray mountain and a gray house for Olivia. Pictures a card for Emily, which is a closed door and a question mark, a gray-blue mound, a sad face hovering above. At 11:00, she turns on the TV, presses + until she gets the Weather Channel, watches all the suns and clouds and maps. There is a blue cloud swirling over Pennsylvania when she hears a clicking in the door, a scraping, and an opening.

*

Hey Em, calls David.

No one answers.

Em? You here? He calls.

He sees Olivia there, in the living room, alone, in the blue glow of the TV.

She turns toward him when he enters, then turns back toward the TV.

He can see her hand is red and raw and bursting open.

The smell hits him as he moves down the hallway: sweet-tinged rotting meat.

Like leaking pipes, he wants to think.

He looks back at Olivia, still sitting in the blue glow.

He wonders, how the hell could she just sit there?

How the hell could she just sit there with that smell?

*

Poor thing. I really don't know how she did it.

An emergency responder wraps a thin, light silver sheet around Olivia. The sheet makes crinkled breaths. Olivia breathes in and out and in. The crinkled sheet makes gentle whispers with her breathing.

I really don't know how you do it. I could never do it, someone says to David, who is standing on the side of his front lawn, holding a white styrofoam cup he does not drink from, watching as the trained professionals are working on Olivia.

*

Meanwhile, on the sixth floor of the high-rise, it is quiet. The full light of the afternoon begins to hit the town. It hovers blue-bright for an hour before turning pale gray, then blushing lavender, as though the clouds are blooming.

The blooms give way to a golden glow, a warm light that makes everything look like an old, hand-tinted postcard photograph. You can see the whole town, laid out in an album of itself. There are the textile mills.

There are the slopes of coal.

There are the red brick buildings and the blonde brick movie theater, and the churches with their lovely, shining copper crowns.

There are the cool white clapboard houses with their grate-fence yards, their shingled roofs, all sloped along the edges of the hills.

A low drone whispers, like the waking of an organ, or the wings of many mourning doves trapped in the rafters of a church, except the whisper isn't trapped above the space where bodies once stood, droning prayers, but underneath, under the space we like to call the ground.

The low drone goes,

> *hmmm, hmmm, hmmm,*
>> *hmmm, hmmm, hmmm,*
>>> *hmmm, hmmm, hmmm,*
>> *hmmm, hmmm, hmmm,*
> *hmmm, hmmm, hmmm,*

A sort of undulating moaning.
Sucking deep lungfuls of gas.
Until its lungs are full.
And it exhales fire.

The fire says, I know, we are a family, I know, we are a family, I know we are, we are, I know, I know, we know, we are, we know, we are, we are, we are, we know, a family, goodbye, goodbye, goodbye, goodbye, goodbye.

Like all the buildings in this town, the old high school has been many things. Before it was a school, it was a hospital. During the year of Spanish flu, they set up rows of metal beds in what would be the classrooms and the auditorium.

Can you imagine?

Lying in a bed, inside the not-yet-finished future school, inside a line of coughing sheeted forms—your neighbors, relatives—as nurses milled around in masked faces, as men came in with cots to cart the covered forms away.

And as the building changed, so did its purpose—beds cleaned, bodies rotated—and every angle of the space was used.

And as afflicted residents surrendered to the flu, the basement of the high school hospital became the morgue.

*

And as they used to say, time marched on, so the beds were shuffled out, the floors were swept, the necessary desks and chairs installed, chalkboards and benches, skinny bathroom stalls, a pool, a piano, and a grand stage framed in velvet drapes, carved wood, and milk glass lamps.

*

The now decaying former school is a little bit of everything, a site for AA meetings, photoshoots, and school plays. The auditorium is staged with props from Phantom of the Opera: candelabras dripped with wax, a family tomb.

Most of the props are real remnants that come with the scenery: the grand piano with its now thick coat of dust, sitting before the stage.

The filtered greenish light, so filled with expectation.

Something in the rafters.

Strange, sad calls.

The fluttering of wings.

*

The man who owns the building leads you on a tour, showing the front rooms where he's re-installed electric lighting, replaced all the panel glass. Although, of course, he has to keep replacing it whenever people in the town throw bricks and stones. He walks the hallways of uprooted boards, paint flecks in ashy, pastel piles, opening the doors to classrooms filled with moss and dripping ceilings. Here's a chalkboard labeled Mrs. Cuff—she's still alive, the owner says—a desk strewn with report cards which, he says, people still ask for.

There is a tiny alcove room, a little metal frame that you must duck under—and almost crawl into—to enter. The room is empty, but the owner says when he first found it, there were pillows, folded bedding, and a child's crib.

*

There is the basement level with a gym—the former morgue—which used to be piled ceiling-high with garbage, says the owner.

There is the half-tile, half-dirt swimming pool, dark closets filled with boxes, bags. All storage, he says, for evicted residents.

*

There is the sound of an old scratchy mewling coming from a closet room that he has set up with a litter box, soft blankets, heating lamps. A bony, matted cat walks toward you in a wavy line, collapses in a wet mound, purring, drooling down his chest.

That's Sam, the owner says. Almost eighteen. He had a few too many accidents back at the house. So, he lives here.

You stroke Sam's chin.

He quivers, sneezes slime.

You get a slick palm, which you wipe along the wall.

II

THE BITTERSWEET

[...] even pleasure can be a crime, especially
once it's lost, and happiness, the word an assault on the tongue,
why, the patient asks the doctor, does everything taste bitter
as the stems of dandelions, even the tongue tasting itself tastes
bitter.

—Diane Seuss, "[Takes time to get to minimalism, years lived
through, eau de]"

When Helen remembers the town, she begins with its absences: a small list of the buildings that were not there, then. The discount stores. The chain gas stations where young people congregate. The brick high-rise, so tall and plain and brown. She pictures summer weekend afternoons. The sun white-hot, the air that smells like paper, and her mother in her gingham apron. She remembers the sound of the hard-bristled broom on the floor—*whisk whisk whisk whisk*—sweeping the coal dust into small piles, out the front door and the back.

Those were the afternoons her dad would always take her out for ice cream. They'd walk hand-in-hand along the sidewalks, underneath the row homes, past the brightly-painted mural of the town, past all the diners: Benny's, Harry's, Janie's, Jimmy's, and Darlene's.

On warm dry days, each block had its own smell.

Fried onions.

Fresh tomato sauce.

Hot cheese and garlic.

And the ice cream parlor, which smelled like the flavors melded into one strong melting, milky sweetness: maplechoconillastrawberbutterfreezerburn.

Meghan Lamb

They'd sit on stools like metal mushrooms, breathing in the sweetness as the fans buzzed and the blenders hummed and rattled, read the chalkboard menu:

Chocolate	Vanilla
Maple Nut	Banana
Butter Brittle	Walnut
Black Raz	Coffee
Coco Cream	Teaberry
	Bittersweet

But they would always get the same. He'd get what they called a *wet walnut* sundae: two big scoops of ice cream, sprinkled walnuts, and a metal spoon of syrup held above it all, drizzling drips of hot sauce, leaving steamy streaks of sweetness in the ice cream. She'd get the *bittersweet*: a perfect blend of plain vanilla mixed with tiny shreds of dark chocolate, the kind her mother used for baking. Every bite was true to its description—sweet and bitter—as she sat and licked and looked down at the green flecks in the tile floor.

*

And every year—that smell, that heat—stirs useless memories and longings. Every morning—waking up, already half-baked. How the heat—the haze, the shimmer of the dust—becomes its own air, its own atmosphere, its own dumb fog, its own dumb hum of almost-hope.

*

Today, the air is warm and dry and thick with dust, still filled with that old paper smell, but tinged with something sour-sweet. Helen opens all the windows to air out the house, which doesn't really work because the smell is everywhere.

She rolls her sleeves up, mixes vinegar to clean the bathroom, dips a sponge, and swipes the counters with their swirls of teal laminate. She digs her nails, scrubbing uselessly at grime- encrusted crevices where dark bits have been gathering for fifty years. She scours the bathtub, with its pale teal porcelain, the ominous black cracks, thinking—as always—that looks bad.

The tub gets clogged—as always—and she has to jerry-rig a wire hanger, bend, and scrape around on scummy elbows.

The stuff she pulls up is ungodly: a long train of hairy slime that dangles down the full length of the hanger, like the tail of some nether creature living on their leavings, in the dark pipes, in the bowels of their house.

*

She shudders.

Rinses off her hands.

Dabs at her eyelids in the mirror.

Her hair's already sweaty and her head aches.

She pulls it all together in a ball and rubber-bands it back.

Her dad cries, Nellie. Nellie.

You need something, Dad? She calls.

She wipes her forehead, squinting in the mirror. She can see a small zit fusing with a wrinkle by her eye.

Do we have ice cream? He says.

I don't know. Just wait a minute.

She leans forward and tries to pop the zit.

The skin bulges and quivers, like it wants to burst, gets bright red, dark red, bulging bigger, harder, bursts, and bleeds.

She wipes her fingers, swipes a stream of water on her face, which is now oozing and now broken and now gross.

*

She shuffles to the kitchen. Opens up the freezer. Sticks her head into the icy droning dark box. She looks.

No ice cream. Sorry, Dad.

She hears him sigh.

You're hot in there?

He says, it's hot.

Hold on a sec. I'll get something to drink, she calls.

She grabs a plastic cup, fills it with filtered water from the fridge. She measures out a tablespoon of Thick-It powder, stirs until the water's the consistency of honey. That's the phrase she always thinks of: *the consistency of honey*. It's what they taught her as a nursing aide, though that was almost thirty years ago.

Her dad is sitting up in bed among his nest of pillows, looking out the open window, breathing in the air.

Feels like another hot one. Yep. He smacks his mouth.

She sets the cup down on his bedside table. Here you go, Dad. Drink your water.

He picks it up and looks into the cup. I hate this stuff.

She laughs. It's water, Dad.

You know, he says, this syrup-water stuff. I always think it will be sweet.

She smiles. It isn't sweet.

He shakes his head. He sips, swallows it down, and makes a face.

I had a craving for that ice cream with the bits, he says. Them little bits. What was it called? That ice cream with the bits.

I think you mean the bittersweet, she says. That's what you mean?

Ah. Yep. I think that's what I mean, he says. The bittersweet.

Those little bits would get stuck in your throat, she says.

He finishes his water, sets it down. Ah. Nah. They melt.

Helen adjusts his pillow and she takes his cup. She shakes her head.

Her father coughs, and sighs. Them little bits don't melt in time.

*

By 9:00, the sour-paper air begins to smell sulfuric, and the house is yellow-warm and shimmering with dust. Helen sweeps the floors out with the same broom that her mother used, now chipped with missing bristles, more than worse for wear.

Her head is pounding as she pours her father's medicine and stirs it in the applesauce and watches the pills sink into its slush, repeating their names, numbly, in her mind, like some enchanted language: oxycodone, allopurinol, lisinopril...

*

She makes their breakfast, eggs with grits. She scrapes her eggs—

crisp and hard—to the side. She makes her dad's eggs soft and scrambled. Makes their coffee—black for her, thickened with sugar stirred-in for her dad—and sets it on a plastic tray. It is the same tray they used for her mom before she died: pale teal, full of thin white strips that mix in with the knife scratches.

She has to make two trips to bring it to him, balancing the tray up two long flights of steep, zig-zagging stairs, which creak precariously, from the dark green forest carpet of the living room, up to the olive shag green carpet of the upstairs hall.

Helen sets the tray beside the bed. She sits next to him in a metal folding chair and sips her coffee, scrapes her egg.

He takes his coffee, swallows, ah. He chuckles.

What's so funny? Helen asks.

He says, I don't remember what my coffee used to taste like.

She turns his bedroom TV on to EWTN, the only channel that he ever watches in the morning. It is a re-run of a sermon preached by Fulton Sheen. The bishop smiles sternly, with that strange false lilt, that sharp face, those stern eyebrows.

Helen swallows, stiffens in her chair.

The bishop hovers in a room with grayish marble walls, an urn of sickly yellow roses soft-focused behind him.

I was talking on adversity—he fake-lilts with his black eyes— and I once used the example of flowers. Some flowers prosper only in the sunshine. Some others seem to thrive only in shade, like fuchsias. A woman came to me after and said, what a wonderful sermon! First time in my life I knew what was wrong with my fuchsias!

*

Helen carries the dishes back downstairs to the kitchen, sets them by the sink. She runs the water hot, breathing its steam. She squirts the bright lime soap. The pipes groan, and she shuts her eyes. She stirs her hands, remembering that awful church, that awful organ sound. That aching echo of so many people standing, murmuring in unison. The chords that sent a deep chill through her bones.

Dressing in the same clothes each week: Helen in her butter-yellow bunting, Helen's mother in her plain-green sheath—nothing too flashy—Helen's father in his double-breasted suit, which set her on edge with its strange divisions, vacancies, a suit made for a second head. The priest was like that too, so terribly severe in all the dull hums of his voice, his half-dead movements, stiff hands clasped beneath his waist. She had to sit and struggle hard to not imagine what was underneath his hands, under his hands, under his hands...She can recall the vestibule: red carpet, glass cases of relics, and a brass-trimmed altar made entirely of coal. A sacred altar, as they spoke of it, because it was one of the very few things that somehow survived the fire. Most of the church was rebuilt, parts assembled from the bits of other churches that had to close down, over the years. The Byzantine-style stations of the cross from the Ukrainians. The giant wooden crucifix from the Italians.

It chills her, even now, remembering that crucifix, not so much from the violence of the nails, or the blood, but from the sickly yellow pallor of Christ's skin, the glazed eyes, and the weirdly tattered linens, like the worn sash of a bathrobe.

*

Helen pulls out a set of day clothes from her father's dresser, sets them on the top, and drapes his robe over his walker. She pulls the walker over to him, helps him out of bed, and watches as he shuffles slowly to the bathroom.

Just cleaned the tub, she says. So sorry if it smells like vinegar.

Probably needed it, her dad says. Hope it wasn't too much trouble.

He smells bad, she thinks, smoothing his sheets, her fingers sweeping up and down the edges where his body rumpled them—*swish swish swish swish*—smoothing the waves of the unnameable smells of an old man, sharp and soft, and strangely sour, somehow, in their softness.

The smell reminds her, she forgot to change the towels.

She gets a clean one from the closet, knocks three times against the closed door.

Tap, tap tap.

Her father cracks the door and reaches out a pale hand.

She passes him the towel, looking down, and turns away.

*

Helen creaks back down to the living room. The voice of Fulton Sheen drains through the hallway, through the stairs, a droning, lilting drizzle. She turns on the living room TV. The next few days bring even hotter weather, full sun graphics and lines of wavy haze.

The yellowed light seeps through the paper blinds and through the diamond window on the front door, casting shadows on the wallpaper: a faded parchment color with a sort of teal toile, which

Helen thought looked very dignified when she was just a girl. It's peeling now, of course. The weather doesn't help. The room is sweltering and dust-thick, bright bits gleaming everywhere. She coughs. She can't imagine how her mother kept things clean, for all those years, keeping her hair pinned in those small, dry, tidy curls.

An idiotic headline draws Helen's attention to the screen: *Local Doctor's Pill Mill Kills Five*. She leans in. She turns the volume up. His patients called him doc, says the reporter in a sing-song voice. The top pain pill prescriber in the state. The candy man.

A tearful woman says, I hope this piece of garbage rots.

A tall man with a thin face says, folks like me suffer every day. We need these pills to just get by. He gave them to us. Now, without him, we're all gonna have an awful nothing-life.

The screen cuts to the white-haired doctor standing in the courtroom, in a gray suit, both hands folded humbly in front of him.

The judge asks, do you understand your right to silence?

The doctor gravely nods. He says, I do.

The pipes shriek, suddenly. The toile wallpaper groans, and something buzzes coldly in the back of Helen's throat. She turns the volume down and listens to the hum around her, feels on edge, as though she's been caught doing something wrong.

*

The dust sticks to her sweat.

She sweeps, again.

She puts away the dishes.

Pays the bills. Speaks to the automated voice that mingles with the mumble of the news, of Fulton Sheen, of her own aching head.

She tells it, make a payment.

No.

Repeat the menu.

Make a payment.

No.

*

The afternoon wanes and she gives herself permission to sit on the porch and smoke her single daily cigarette. She sits down on the concrete steps, angling low so she does not blow any smoke onto her neighbors' porches. She turns the box upside-down in her palm and taps the bottom, turns it right-side up, and slides a cigarette into her hand. She holds it for a moment, contemplates how strange it is, this little stick of weeds and chemicals, all paper-mummified.

She lights it, breathes. The smell blends with the air. She hears the barking of some distant dog, the crackle of some distant kid pedaling up the sidewalk with his plastic wheels. She looks over the row of houses, angled sharp up the hill, like old teeth cutting through the asphalt.

There is the house that still has all its Christmas decorations, crisping in the sun. There is the house that has the taxidermied fox, pressed up against the window with its frozen frightened look. The house with three slab-sections of a roof, in shades of tin-rust, beige, and black. There are the signs on many doors along this street, and others, which she knows are there. She thinks about them, sometimes. Sometimes, she forgets. Official signs that say:

Failure to Thrive

Danger: Oxygen in Use
Danger: Oxygen in Use
Danger: Oxygen in Use

*

The afternoon drifts by.

She turns on the old box fan and it rattles, blowing dust. She sweeps the dust. She dabs the sweat drops from her forehead with her sticky shirt. She plays a lazy game of Go Fish with her father, which of course she always lets him win.

He says, but Nellie, Nellie, you were always good at games.

She shakes her head. I'm no good really, Dad. I never have been. That was Mother.

*

She sweeps the dust, again. And then, it's time for dinner. Suddenly. And finally. She opens up the freezer, stands, heat hovering, a halo in the still cold of the dark hum of the black box, until she feels cool and calm, prepared to end the day.

She takes two frozen meals, opens them, and microwaves. Spoons his onto a plate: an oval mound of corn, an oval mound of mashed potatoes, beige and brown-flecked slab of chicken, which she cuts in inch-sized bits. Another long-held habit from her long-ago-held job.

She carries up the teal tray and sets it on the bedside table, mutes the TV, asks, how are you doing, Dad?

Oh, can't complain, he says. Just hot.

She nods.

He takes his plate and sighs, I have a taste for that ice cream. Sometimes you get a taste, know what I mean?

She does.

She says, I do. We had some good times in that ice cream shop.

He chews and swallows. Place to go, when it gets hot.

Supposed to stay this way, awhile, she says.

He shakes his head, as though in disbelief. Somebody tell the sun, we seen enough.

The news is on. Another headline for that story: *Local Doctor Prescribed Thousands of Illegal Opioids.*

Her father chews, watches without speaking.

She chews, watching him watch the news, their stomachs growling softly at each other.

*

The day is done. The light is gray. The house is quiet.

She wanders, looking through the windows, carrying a glass of water. She feels like she's waiting for something, or waiting something out, or maybe merely checking to make sure nothing gets in. She stands inside her room, the same since she was ten: that rose-print paper with bright olive stems that match the old shag carpet. From the window, in the corner, just beyond the farthest chimney, she can see the dark brown brick edge of the high-rise.

Helen sips her water, climbs the little half staircase up into the alcove room that's always been more or less empty. The paneled walls are bowing out in several places. Probably a cracked foundation. She stopped caring years ago.

She grips the window sash, glancing down at the sticker with the set of strange instructions she has never bothered to remove.

ATTENTION

After returning sash
to upright position,
always first raise
the sash - then
lower it. If sash
cannot raise,
tilt sash out
to 90° again
and return
upright.

She opens the window. From here, she has a great view of the graveyard sprawled across the mountain top, sloping precariously. She sees the blonde grass, badly overgrown, the brown silk flowers, and she smirks. She knows—in a way, has always known—what is wrong with her fuchsias. Across from her, another big house stands, streaked gray with dust. The windows dark. Abandoned. Screen mesh torn and flapping like a flag.

She sips her water. Finishes her glass.

She tilts the sash out to 90°, again.

Returns upright.

*

And every night—this time of year—she gets a taste, oh, just the slightest taste of all this soft warmth, all this lightness, heavy in the dim-glow, what she could be feeling—or, maybe, unfeeling—unremembering—or, unimagining—oh, just the slightest taste—the bittersweetness—just a little softening of all of what's already there, around her: all the soft, dark warmth, a small bite of oblivion.

*

Helen opens her eyes, slowly, to the red blur that begins to firm itself into a set of red, digital dashes. The dashes read, 3:36. She rubs her eyelids, rises out of bed.

Over the years, she's trained herself to wake at some point in the night. She goes to check in on her father while he's sleeping. She runs her hand along the wall, balancing, creaking, in the dark. Her father's snoring fills the whole house with its rumbled wheeze.

A sucking rattle of a groan.

Hmmm-nnnnn.

A crackled exhale.

Kkkkkk-ahhhhh.

A dry, sharp whisper-whistle.

Shhheeeee!

She squints into the hall as she steps closer to her father's door. She feels the strange half-anxious, half-hope she will see something, that this will be the night when something happens, something changes.

She pulls the cracked door open wider, peers in.

Nothing.

Just a small shape rising softly, making sounds inside the bed.

Hmmm-NNNNN.

Kkkkk-AHHHHH.

SHHEEEEEE!

She gently creaks across the hallway, to her own room.

Lowers herself down into the bed, kicks back the sheets.

She lies there in the dark, awhile.

Trying not to listen.

Listening.

Trying not to listen.

Listening.

She reaches underneath her nightgown, runs her hand along her ribcage.

Shuts her eyes, tight.

Trying not to listen.

Listening.

Her hand moves down her stomach.

Flutters, hesitantly.

Hovers over her wet hair, as if she's waiting, waiting for someone's permission.

And her answer is...

Hmmm-NNNNN.

Kkkkk-AHHHHH.

SHHEEEEEE!

*

Her alarm goes off at 7:00 am, as it always does, but she is up already, sweeping out the dust. Her father starts to stir at 7:30, yawning, coughing, calling out, it's gonna be another hot one, Nellie!

She cracks the last eggs with a tinge of apprehension, knowing this will be the day she has to venture to the grocery store. Today is Sunday, she thinks. I'll make sure that I get out by 9:00, when everyone in town is still at church.

She brings the buttered grits, eggs, coffee.

He sips, sighs. I wish we had that ice cream.

Helen shakes her head. You mean, you wish that you *could* have it.

He smiles, straining all the lines around his eyes. Do you remember what your mother used to tell you about wishing?

She nods, knowingly, and they both drone in unison:

Wish in one hand.

Shit in the other.

See which piles up faster.

He clicks his tongue. She *was* a personality, he says.

She nods, never quite knowing what that means, if she agrees, which is to say, not knowing what it means to *be* a personality, and if it is the same as having one.

*

Helen takes a towel from the hallway closet, strips down in the bathroom, folds her clothes and sets them on the old wall shelves. They all still have the contact paper that her mother added in the 70s: blue daisies, faded flecks of green.

Still smells like vinegar. She cracks the window. Sour-paper air. She runs the bath hot, even though it's summer, steaming up the mirror. Good. She doesn't want to see her sagging breasts, her wrinkle-zits, her sad-sack face—an okay face, though, really—

yes, a face that's always been okay. But just okay. She doesn't want to look and wonder, is it good enough—still good enough—for what, she doesn't know.

She eases down into the half-empty, half-full bath, staring at her stomach rolls, thinking, okay, okay, wish in one hand...

*

I'm going out, she tells her father when she's dried off and put on a clean skirt with a t-shirt long enough to cover the elastic band.

He looks at her. He looks at what she's wearing and he makes a face.

She says, it's *hot*.

He says, you know, it's *Sunday*.

She nods, knowing, of course, what he would like for that to mean.

I won't be gone too long, she tells her father, softly.

She switches on EWTN as she leaves. Back behind her, seeping through the stairs, she hears some strange, shrill cartoon voice intoning lines she recognizes from Psalm 22: They have pierced my hands and my feet! I can count all my bones!

*

Helen pulls the car out from the parked line all along the row homes, starts her drive taking a deep dive down the hill. The engine rattles the small tooth-white flat beads of her mother's rosary, which quivers, lightly, from the rear-view mirror.

She passes by the high-rise, sees a pair of old men smoking, sitting side-by-side on benches on the concrete porch. She sees a woman wearing teal scrubs exiting toward the parking lot. Nursing assistant, likely from her former agency.

She passes Benny's, Harry's, what used to be Janie's, what is maybe still Darlene's but never looks like it is open, and the local market, and the discount store that doesn't have the best discounts, both places, anyhow, where she might see someone she knows. She rolls the window down. The air feels good. The hills are green and lovely. It's a nice day, not too hot yet, not too bright. With a little effort from her own imagination, she feels like she could be going anywhere. But then, she sees the old sign from the Pine Burr Inn, bearing the daily special—PBI scramble—and knows exactly where she is.

*

She pulls off at the Walmart, finds a shady spot, and parks her car toward the back side of the building. She gets in through the sliding doors, already has a map in her mind of the items that she needs, where she can find them in the store. Up one aisle, down another, up one aisle, down another, in a calculated zig-zag through her list.

eggs + milk	Aisle 1
peas	Aisle 3
bread + potato flakes	Aisle 4
pasta + oil	Aisle 5
water + soda	Aisle 6
dish soap + detergent	Aisle 7
paper towels + TP	Aisle 8

She sees a woman, maybe her age, walking with a younger woman who is humming, touching all the items on each shelf. She sees a young worker, sitting down on the floor, attempting to arrange the pillows on the low shelves in neat stacks.

The pillows in their slick, clear plastic bags slip down.

The worker picks them up and tries again.

They just keep slipping down.

*

When she gets out, the sun is white-hot, and the paper smell wraps all around as if the sky were covered with an old tarpaulin. An AC unit hums while unseen insects buzz, burrowed in broken concrete bowls of yellow weeds. Gray waves of dust drift through the parking lot. The town takes on a pale, gray-gold haze, like an old photograph. The haze makes Helen hungry for the bittersweet ice cream. She gets behind the wheel, wipes her forehead, wipes her hand off on her skirt. Touches her fingertips—just barely—to her mother's rosary.

She drives back down the highway, past the Pine Burr Inn, past Pool World: a lot of dingy, faded teal tubs that no one ever buys. She zig-zags down the hill, then up another, past shit-creek, past all the bars and clubs inside their old dark-windowed houses. The rosary goes *tap, tap, tap*—the high-rise in her rear-view—as she drives past Janie's, Jimmy's and Darlene's. She parks her car along the next block, where the ice cream parlor is just opening to serve their Sunday breakfast special.

The smell of frozen sugar mixed with stale grease, the green-flecked floor, the metal mushroom stools. The same cooler—as always—full of bittersweet. Helen picks out a pint and pays the counter waitress, who nods when she smiles. Thank you. Welcome.

As she walks through the door, she sees a family coming in: a tan teenage girl slouched over her phone, an uncomfortable-looking young man, an attractive black man in a button-down shirt, and a brittle-haired white woman in a frothy summer dress. Helen's heart jumps then because she recognizes her: a worker from her former nursing agency.

The woman offers a weak smile with a weary little head tilt, like her sympathies cannot extend beyond her strange stiff hair. Helen can feel her own mouth muscles twitching in a sort of mild pain, in what she must assume is the equivalent.

*

Back home, EWTN is blaring as she brings the bags in, sets them on the counter, begins putting things away. A low-voiced priest intones: And the Father who sent me has himself borne witness to me. His voice you have not heard. His form you have not seen.

I got the bittersweet, she calls out to her father.

He does not answer.

Hey, Dad?

No answer. She puts down her bag and climbs the stairs.

She finds him sleeping in his bed, somehow. His chest is rising, falling, rising, falling, but his face is strange and soundless, motionless. He is an open-mouthed mound, white-washed by a beam of light, wrapped in a shroud of blankets.

She turns the volume down low, taps his shoulder.

Dad, you turned the volume up too high again.

He squints. You back already?

She says, you want some ice cream?

He rubs his eyes and chuckles. I don't know. Is water wet?

Helen takes the opportunity to change the channel to the local news. It's kids promoting back-to-school fundraisers. She creaks downstairs into the kitchen, peels off the ice cream lid, and takes a tiny spoonful for herself.

She lets the plain vanilla ice cream melt into her tongue, and waits until the bitter bits turn warm before she swallows.

She scoops the rest into the blender. Puts it on puree. Adds in a dash of Thick-It powder: *the consistency of honey*. Pours the mix into a big ceramic bowl she always loved when she was little, filled with stars and pastel polka dots.

She carries it up to her father, sets it on his bedside table.

He looks down, looks up, offers a light shrug.

He takes a bite and churns it over in his mouth.

He presses his lips into a thin line, considering.

He takes another bite and shakes his head.

She says, it's not the same, is it? She sighs.

Ah no, he says. It's not the same.

*

Helen goes out to the porch and sits down on the concrete steps. She takes a neon orange popsicle, a box of cigarettes. She lights one, licks one, holding them in alternating hands. Breathes orange burning paper. Wet, cold lips. Hot air. Cracked pavement. Barking dog. Fried decorations. Licks and licks. Sips in more dirty air. Breathes out sweet clouds, looking off at an angle, at the coal-gray smudges on the clapboard. Dust and dust. Gets to the always awkward moment of the popsicle, the part where all the orange is too low-down on the stick to reach with just her mouth, and she must make a choice: either bite fast, directly into ice, or shove the stick deep down her throat. She picks the latter, gives herself a quick choke-shock of orange ice, and sucks a hard hiss, so it slides off, and she swallows it.

She thinks about the church, the altar made of coal, the sickly face of Jesus on the cross, the voices of the congregation murmuring:

The Lord be with you.	And also with you.
The Word of God.	Thanks be to God.
Lord, have mercy.	Lord, have mercy.
Christ have mercy.	Christ have mercy.

She remembers how she moved her mouth without speaking, without forming the words, afraid of some enchantment in them. She breathes in, thinking of the parchment flavor of the eucharist, placed on her tongue. Exhales sticky smoke rings. She stubs her cigarette out on the step and sweeps the small pile from the past few days off down the angle of the sidewalk. In the distance, she can see the top floors of the high-rise. She can see the windows, small white dots of AC units, drawn shades.

It looks the same as it did thirty years ago, when Helen was so happy to be hired by the agency. She was a young thing, just excited to start saving for her own apartment, for a space with no one else's name on it. She knew, even then, she was no one special. But she had no special needs, no impossible desires. Just a girl with young, bright energy, a yearning to be useful, to be independent, competent, and capable.

She had vague aspirations to save money, to move elsewhere. But then, the job was not what she thought it would be. The rooms were small and sad. The hours were short, but they felt long. The clients were not kind. Well, some were sometimes funny, like the man who thought they were in Poland, or the man who always asked if she was Uke-a-ranian. But mostly, they saw her for what she was—and what she knew she was—shifting these brittle skins, these poor sore bones, always just on the verge of breaking. She'd get pinched, or kicked, or twisted by the residents, and she would have to swallow, deep, and try her best not to react. She'd get snapped at by snippy bitches who were ultimately right in their assessment: You don't know what you're doing, do you?

And as the job started to wear on her, so did the town. She noticed the unpleasantness of her surroundings everywhere. The raw facade of the old dress factory, peeling out onto the street. The streets themselves, all sharp and jagged, houses jutting from the hills. The paper smell. The old pea soup smell of the tower. Peoples' teeth in jars. The smell of rotting food and pickles in the fridge. She needed something, just to soften all the edges. So she told herself. Or so she told her parents, when the agency had to investigate. The start of a long process that she never did recover from. That they never recovered from.

And so, now, here she is.

Helen shuts her eyes.

Her head hurts.

She taps out another cigarette from the pack and lights it.

Breathes in, breathes out, breathes in, breathes out in sticky bitter little clouds, attempting to ignore the smell.

What would she be doing, right now, if she had moved out?

Helen pictures a small house in a small neighborhood where everything is flat and clean. She pictures herself in a pair of pastel scrubs, a real nurse who went to college, graduated, moved on up the ladder of her life without any missteps, which is to say, looking ahead, not looking at the wrong things—looking down.

*

She sweeps the dust.

She opens cabinets and drawers.

She puts away the dishes and utensils.

She turns the mugs so all the handles face in.

She pushes down the curled-up edges of her mother's contact lining.

*

Helen makes her father's dinner: buttery potato flakes with canned peas, stirred into a dish of gray-green mush. She makes a peanut butter sandwich for herself, slices the sandwich into triangular halves, the way her mother used to.

She sets the tray down on the bedside table, notices her father looks pale.

Do you feel okay? She asks.

His eyes look glazed. His mouth opens and hovers for a moment, questioning, before he can admit to her, Nellie, I hurt.

Helen smoothes back his hair. I'll bring you up a pain pill, once you've eaten.

Her father draws a dry breath. He says, one.

Just one, Helen agrees.

He looks at her like he's about to say something else.

But he doesn't, and they both finish their food.

*

The screen then darkens with the shape of Fulton Sheen, here in full bishop's cloak, his eyebrows furrowed, hands clasped hard in front of him. He stares coldly into the static of the screen, looking out, looking through it, out through space, and time, directly into Helen's eyes.

Fulton Sheen says, friends. As our subject is Women Who Do Not Fail, I would like to tell the oldest story about women, and against them.

The story is of Adam, after the fall of man.

He was walking one day with his two boys, Cain and Able.

They passed the wreck and ruin of the once beautiful garden of paradise.

Adam looked in rather wistfully.

He pulled the two boys to himself and then said, boys: that's where your mother ate us out of house and home.

*

Some other version of Helen—never quite seen, or shaped, or accessed—rolls her eyes at this ridiculous expression. The rolling eyes of this un-accessed Helen—swallowed deep—feel like two milky marbles churning bile in her stomach. Who is he, after all, with his fake lilt, his jaundiced-looking face, his caterpillar eyebrows, and his ugly maggot mouth? Her mother would agree, if she were still alive. Her father would agree, most likely, if her mother would. But she cannot. And he cannot. And Helen does not roll her eyes—the real one, the one who never made it anywhere— and she feels chilled even within the heat, her shoulders shrinking down, feeling the full weight of the wreck and ruin falling on her, pressing on her, crushing her.

*

But, as her mother always said: time marches on.

And as her mother always said, maybe more to the point: It takes less time to do something the right way than to explain why it was done wrong.

*

She sweeps the dust. She opens, closes windows, turns the rickety old box fan on, and off, and listens to it blowing. The air gets colder, stronger, and she puts the fan away. She hears her father coughing, and she hears his cough grow hoarser, louder. She looks over the graveyard, the abandoned house. The old screen fibers, flapping. Helen shuts the windows, draws the curtains down over the final days of summer.

ATTENTION

After returning sash
to upright position,
always first raise
the sash - then
lower it. If sash
cannot raise,
tilt sash out
to 90° again
and return
upright.

*

When Helen wakes up, she is cold. Her hands, particularly. She rubs them together, blows into her palms, and clasps her fingers like she's praying. And perhaps she is, if you believe that praying is only a way to try to hold a little warmth inside your hands. Her father coughs an awful rattle, like an underground machine, a cold dark crackling of liquid that stays deep and buried in his lungs. She makes a little runny mound of grits and eggs. She pours his half into the blender, sets it on puree. Pours in a half-cup of warm water, a whole tablespoon of thickener, until *it's the consistency of honey*. And perhaps it is a kind of honey, if you can believe honey is pale yellow-sick and smells like sulfur.

*

Her father's sheets are damp, again, and he is shivering. She puts on gloves to change them, rolls him over on his side. He winces. She can see it, even though he tries to hide it.

She knows where to look. She has a keen sense of his frailty.

I'm sorry, Dad, she says. She hates the bed roll, always hated it. She's never really done it right. No, she was never good at this.

She bundles up the sheets, holds them away from her. She carries them into the laundry closet, sets them in their hamper, one of three in her new system:

1. dirty linens
2. dirty dry clothes
3. dirty piss or shit-soiled

*

Helen drives through town because they need detergent, soap, and dryer sheets—Aisle 7—and more paper towels—Aisle 8. It is a thick gray morning. Strands of fog curl through the mountains, through the branches of the trees, the dark green pines, the brown and yellow leaves.

Her headlights beam, lighting the white lines of the road, the fringes of the branches, just the barest edges of the buildings, and the tall sign of the Pine Burr Inn, which reads:

Breakfast - Daily - 8am
Cold Beer TO GO
Funeral Dinner - Friday 6pm

*

She breezes past Aisles 1, 2, 3, 4, 5, 6. Stops at 7.

Hovers for a moment, half-concealed by the shelves.

She sees her old boss from the agency, clack-clacking with her metal cart.

And all the air inside her body freezes in her chest.

Helen's old boss looks small and whitewashed in a pale, off-white shirt—beneath the off-white lights—and off, somehow: shorter than she remembered. Standing on her tiptoes, batting at a high box, fingers scraping at the edges of the shelves.

Her old boss bobs up, down, there, reaching, as though stuck in time, stuck in this motion, caught forever, reaching, in this moment.

And something jolts in Helen.

The fingers going *tap, tap, tap*, like trying to shake hands with something she will never have.

Helen breathes in, presses her lips together, and darts down the aisle, looking down, wishing her hair was not pulled back.

She reaches up. A blue vein bulges in her arm, as though detached from her.

She grabs the high box off the shelf. Shoves it in her old boss's cart.

As Helen speeds off, heart clenched, cold, she hears a soft voice calling down the aisle. Thank you?

Strangely distant, as though years away.

Too weak.

Too late.

Too many years, thinks Helen, heels squeaking as her shoes leave black streak-scratches on the floor.

*

Helen drives back through the mountains, through the fog, now clearing, strangely wary of familiar bits of spaces now revealed.

The blue concavities of Pool World.

The blood-brown-orange shit-creek.

All the figures drifting gloomily around it.

*

At the house, her father cries out, Nellie, Nellie, until his voice trails off, from pain, or from a bad dream, she can't always tell.

It doesn't matter. Helen's remedy remains the same, regardless: applesauce and pills.

And if he still hurts: more pills.

Is it a dark day? Asks her father.

Foggy, Helen says.

He nods. I feel the fog, he says. I've always felt the fog.

I've always felt it too, says Helen, not quite knowing what he means, or if the fog they've felt has always been the same.

*

She lays a towel on the sheets, another towel on his upper body, and undoes his nightshirt, dabs him with a warm, wet cloth. She moves the towel down his body, bit by bit, in an attempt to see as little of her father's parts as possible.

A flash of breast bone.

Flash of gray-pink, fungal nipple.

Flaccid penis.

She looks just long enough to wipe them clean. She scrubs the black grit underneath his nails and she blows on each, to dry them.

He murmurs, Nellie, please. The pan, please. Sorry. Thank you.

She bends down to reach the pan.

She reaches underneath him, clumsy, tired.

She thinks, don't spill it, now, don't spill it, now, you will, you will, you will, you will, you will, spill it, you will, you will, you will, you will spill, you will, you will, you will...

*

She pinches skin.

He hisses, and she flinches, shifts the pan.

She does. She splashes piss.

His dry lids look into her eyes, skin flecked.

And she does not snap, then, so much as seep.

Some inner black whirr she has carried—inner smoke—begins to drain out of her chest, her stomach, in a stream she does not hear or feel coming from her, because—she then realizes—it's not coming from her, but her father, as he slowly breathes in, and exhales in a long, low whisper trail of a sigh that sounds like:
Sheeeeeeeeeeeeeeeeeeeeee...............

*

She swallows.

She looks out the window at the vague gray, at the fog.

She sees it without seeing it: the dark brown outline.

All the rooms inside, a honeycomb, all thick with sickness.

All the half-drawn shades, like fluttered wings of eyelids, shuttering.

*

She strips the sheets, again. She drops them in the hamper, takes the piss pan to the bathroom, drains it down the toilet bowl, and flushes.

She lowers herself, wraps her arms across her folded knees, her bare feet flat against the tile floor, her back pressed up against the tub.

It all still smells like vinegar.

She gets a bitter taste, a tickle in her throat.

She sits there for a long time.

Squinting acid.

Blinking.

Something still inside her.

Something burning in her chest.

The bitterness inside her mouth just builds and builds and builds.

She stands up, stiffly, spits into the sink.

She tilts her head beneath the faucet.

Rinses her mouth with the rust-tinged running tap.

Her head feels numb and dry and dumb and empty.

She laps up the water like a frightened animal.

When she feels full, she stops the tap.

She wipes the tip.

Gray slime. She breathes.

An iron smell, inside the pipes.

Deep and medieval.

A low groaning, like an organ.

A long hum.

A voice-like resonance.

A *drip, drip, drip.*

A *tap, tap, tap.*

And then, the house falls silent.

*

She creaks across the hallway, falls back into bed. She lies there, watching shadows stretch across the paper rose bouquets, like vines. Her father coughs. His cough becomes a harsh snore, wanes into a wheeze.

She realizes, in the not too distant future, he will die.

And I will have no one.

And if I want to, I can leave.

She closes her eyes.

Pictures herself driving down the highway.

Past shit-creek. Past Pool World. Past Walmart.

She can imagine this. The driving. The excitement of the drive.

She can imagine this part, getting out, getting away.

But when she tries to picture where she'd land, she can't imagine anything beyond the outline of a house, the white lines of the road, the headlights as they bend around the mountain— bleeding streams of ice—blending into the darkness of the fog.

*

The smoke of burning leaves.

The charred bits of a church.

The cold chords of a hymn.

The rustling of branches, cracking of a sidewalk.

The sound of voices, circling from some eternal summer dusk.

Ashes, ashes, ashes, and we all...

*

Then, what emerges from the fog is not the future, but a memory. Another day, in autumn, in the week before first grade. Her mother brought home a new back-to-school dress and pulled it out of its brown paper bag for her to try it on.

It was an odd pea-green—synthetic—polka dots and pockets, pointed collar, three big plastic buttons shaped like dinner plates.

Helen inspected the exotic dress and noticed that the tag said it was made in *China*.

Yet, now—somehow—here it was.

All Helen knew about *China* was that it was another country, far away. Her mother helped her find it on a world map. She pointed—*we live here*—and traced her finger through the ocean blue, into a salmon-colored country full of mountains.

Helen looked closer at the map, searching within the space her mother pointed to—*we live here*—but she couldn't find their town.

Where is our town? She asked.

Her mother laughed, and reached across the atlas for the

sewing kit she kept beside the shelf.

She took a skinny needle from the cushion, found the right spot—*tap, tap, tap*—right there, she said, and stuck it in the map.

It stood, a faint flag, teetering inside their state, until a loose thread dangled from the needle's eye and fell into the ocean.

A low drone whispers, like the waking of a tank, turned on, a tank of cold, metallic oxygen, a tank of gas, a wheeze—hack, ack ack ack ack—and then, the whisper of an artificial wind, which sounds like cracked glass, hiss hiss-ssssssssss, a weakening of lungs.

The hiss goes,
> *ashes, ashes, ashes*
>> *and we all*
>> *we all*
> *we all*

The hiss goes
> *round and round*
and round and round
and round
A sort of undulating.
Deep lungfuls of gas.
And now—as usual—its lungs
are flowing,
growing full.
And it exhales fire.

The Concrete City never was a real city, or a town. It was—in modern terms—something like a development: eight concrete blocks of housing built like bunkers for the workers of an old rail company's coal mine division.

*

It has developed, mostly, as an empty space, occasionally filled by teenagers who venture through the woods. Today, you see their remnants: crumpled glints of wrappers, crushed-up cans, and rusted coils of mattresses drug through the cinders, sunk in mud.

The former courtyard is a current of dry grass. A hushed wind, brushing unseen fingertips that turn the unseen pages of an untold tale. A tale that is the gleam of broken bottles, shotgun shells, the seams of stray, stripped garments. Hooded jackets. Skirts.

*

Torn strands of caution tape, of course, that no one heeded. After all, what was the point of being there if not to break things, make things broken?

They left long trails of paint along the roofs. The charred frames of the windows. Vines of twisting branches. Curls of moss.

*

They tagged their names like—Joey, Wes, and Jamie—left each other questions like—Anal? America? They left responses like— hell yeah—or—nah—or—with your mom.

And then, they left taunts for each other in unsteady places. Spaces where the walls caved in, gave way to holes that you could see through. Mountains. Darkness. Spaces where the floors were cracking and collapsing, iron wires dangled like some raw nerves razed with anger.

*

Somebody must have been afraid to use the stairs because they're sprayed with messages like—Oh no! Don't look!—Arrows pointing down.

And then, there is a taunt that spreads itself over the full length of the stairs.

I

  hope

     you

       fall

        and

         die

          you

           faggot

            bitch.

III

THE SLOW BURN

Under the night, somewhere
between the white that is nothing so much as
blue, and the black that is, finally; nothing,
I am the man neither of you remembers.

—Carl Phillips, "Blue"

Jack starts off little, low, down at the bottom of the high hill, looking up, small feet pressed into big wheel pedals, side strips blinking on his velcro shoes, like headlights, sweatpants stuffed in socks, puff jacket zipped, a pale gray sky, horizon to the concrete runway of the sidewalk. He pushes pedals and his big wheel's metal spokes begin to whirr. The plastic crackles over pebbles, flinging bits of dust. He picks up speed, more speed, until he's scraping gusts of upward movement with his wheel, pedals skittering, feet pressing hard. His knees are chugging up and down, and up and down, along, breath in cold clouds, as he blurs through the world, pushing to the top. He sees a ball of barking fuzz. He hears Mrs. Moretti's click-click-clicking shoes, and garbage cans all lined up in their rows, 1, 2, 3, 4, 5, 6, and he is almost there, up to the curb's edge, and his big wheel goes crr-clomp down, crr-crunch, and he's made it. He swerves his handlebars to curve around the block, passing another row of garbage cans, 1, 2, 3, 4, 5, 6, and Mr. Mosser sitting on his porch, and waving, and he nods, but doesn't wave, because he's coming to another curb, crr-crunch. He pedals down another block, the mailbox, the bridge above the neon-orange creek. He turns and whirs around another block, and now the best part, down the hill, cliicliicliiclickleclickclecklicrack lecrackrr-crunch! The up, and down, around the sidewalks, steps, and gates, and garbage cans, and curbs, and barks, and waves, and all the whole blurred neighborhood becomes the morning and most of the afternoon, the tingles of his skin, the chill caught in his lungs, the street, the wind, the sound made by his movement.

*

It seems the whole of Jack's young life goes by like this. At least, that's how he now remembers it. That's how he now remembers. 25 years of the whole blurred world. With small pricks from the strangest things. Like how his little feet pressed into the green turf porch, which left an imprint that would swiftly fade. Like how his mother used to brush her lonely, soap-stiff hands along his cheek—her soap-white hands, her chemical-rose lotion smell— and smooth his own skin searchingly, with words to justify her search, her little nameless sadnesses, like Jack, you need more lotion, you are ashy—dabbing chemical-rose white cream waves to try to fill-in something—smother something—rub the ashes out. The way the house felt huge—the stairway looming steeply over Dad's big chair, the mismatched couch, the rickety old exercise bike no one used—then suddenly felt small as Jack grew taller, as the walls started to sag, sink in around him. The way the town started to feel small the year he graduated from the big wheel to the bike and rode the town's periphery with Gio Costa. Roller-coaster rush of hills. Excitement twisting like some vapid chain around a hard-coiled feeling in his gut. The elementary school halls. The middle school halls. The high school halls. Bright buzzing lights, white bodies pushing past in hooded sweatshirts—which he also wore, along with the few other black and brown kids—trying to blend in, blur through, to not be noticed. The necessary fields, football practice. Locker rooms with metal-sweat smell—which he always loved, of course he still remembers this—the way that smell felt like a chain unlocking from his gut, felt like a whispering unwisping, like a secret stirring in him. An electricity of its own kind, humming beneath the cold sick energy of running, rushing, pushing bodies into bodies. He could hide within this energy, like giving off electric signs of invisible lettering: don't look at me, don't look at me. That all feels blurred, too. Summers hazy, wasted, with his teammates, waiting to see who would leave and who would stay, which is to say, who would get lucky, who would get someone knocked up—although Jack figured out, by then, that he was not at risk in that department. The seasons blurring with the feeling of his first car, an old Jeep that you could roll the top back from to feel the breeze. Long summers stretching into fall, his Jeep, his heat turned up, the top rolled down, a cold wind whipping at his outsides, hot whirs wrapped around his insides. Friends who rode with him, at first. But then, he mostly drove alone. The bleeding out of friends who left. The bleeding of Jack's headlights through the lonely mountain dark, an hour's drive to reach the karaoke bar with over-priced Long Island Iced Teas, rainbow-colored lights.

*

He tries to picture this, now, riding back along the highway, in the backseat of his parent's Oldsmobile, back in time. He tries to picture moments, scenes with clear divisions—a before and after—

tries to organize them chronologically. But what he gets is shades of strong sensation—happiness, excitement, fear—attached to foggy outlines, bodies. Watching gray sky, strip malls, rest stops, Michigan, Ohio, Indiana license plates...

*

Five years ago, Jack drove the old Jeep to Ohio...he remembers this...the landscape getting flatter, duller, easier to drive through.

Things he can remember: Driving. Smoking. Flatness. Grayness. Highway.

His apartment in Ohio. Big gray new build.

He can remember hearing cars at night...

He went to bars, sometimes. Ohio bars felt strange because nobody smoked inside.

It all feels strange, of course. It blurs. And it was all so barely real to begin with.

He had a job, there, came there for a job. A wood furniture factory nearby. He hears the sound of ringing saws.

*

Things he cannot remember: Orders. Ordering of operations. Anything that has more than a few steps of instruction.

He feels blank—and he remembers feeling blank—hearing his supervisors ask him questions, answering. Okay. Okay. Okay. He does remember—can remember—only so much—but he never knows which things will prick him, when, which things he simply won't return. The process of assembly. Process. Ordering of

164

operations. The sensation of what to do with his hands, and when. The blankness getting pricked, then. Hot rush. The embarrassment of knowing he could not stay, doing what he had been doing...

He feels blank. He never knows which things will prick him. Pierce him. Make him feel something. Make him bleed back into being. Make a memory become complete. Or which things will remain deep-down, and dark, and dangerously seeping, blurring altogether.

*

And he remembers almost nothing of the car crash.

He has been told—many times—he was just a few blocks from his place around 3 am.

And a drunk kid in a truck T-boned his Jeep.

And Jack was in a coma for three days.

All he remembers is...

The dark.

A sudden light.

Too bright.

An underwater feeling.

Like his mind was diving down into itself.

A prick of recognition and a sink of resignation.

He remembers that: the sinking feeling.

You're in trouble.

You've been caught.

*

And now, six months have somehow passed, and he is riding in the back seat of his parents' Oldsmobile, his little sister Jasmine sitting next to him, head nodding, headphones pressed around her thick braids, seemingly absorbed there, in her separate world of sound. She's grown up so fast in his absence, Jack thinks, trying to remember her before—a fast-forward montage of dizzy little kid shapes. And he can't help wondering how much has happened in the blurs of time he can't see—hasn't seen—that he's now interrupting.

She's eating from a bag of cherry licorice nibs, filling the whole car with sweet lipstick-ish candy smell. She picks, and nips, and chews one small piece at a time, until she gets frustrated, dumps a sticky, heart-sized, brain-shaped blob into her palm.

Their mother cranes her head around her seat and says—her voice dead serious—Don't you think you should ask Jack if he wants some?

His sister smiles at him shyly. Do you want some? She says, softly.

Jack says, sure. He picks a cluster from the bright red blob.

It's raining sleet. The sky is gray. The road is gray-black slush.

Jack watches drops run down the window, chewing at his licorice.

The chewing makes his cheekbones hurt.

It feels like a lot of work.

The highway slowly starts to curve.

The hills rise into mountains.

The fog grows thick. He sees the pale teal arcs of bridges. Pine trees thinning into birches. Bare sprigs in the snow.

His stomach burns around the hard sweet lumps of licorice.

That vapid chain re-coiling and re-locking all around the secret in his gut.

He sees the old sign of the Pine Burr Inn.

Breakfast - Daily - 8am
Cold Beer TO GO
Deuces X 2

He sees the town begin to spread itself in dusky sheaths of clapboard, streaks of coal, and dirty strands of tinsel, dangling. Christmas decorations everywhere. Old plastic figures with their washed-out faces, reds so faded they look barely pink. Those strands of lights, blinking, on, off, on, off, on, off, making the shapes of everything they're wrapped around—coiled over, under—look unreal. Animated. Jack rubs at his eyes, looking out through the window drops. The drunk haze of the lights. This fucked up cartoon world.

And here they come. Now, past the churches with their crowns. The old shit-creek, the orange water churning foils of trash into acidic rust balls of debris. Now, down the hill—which seems not quite as steep—the garbage cans lined, 1, 2, 3, 4, 5, 6, gray, cracked concrete, moonish cratered siding, strips of astroturf, Mrs. Moretti smoking on her porch, a dim-lit, little gray-glazed silhouette.

There is a red sign with a white X nailed to Mr. Mosser's house. Jack notices the house is dark.

Boards over all the windows.

*

Now, past the door. Now, past Dad's big chair, which now has a piece of duct tape stuck over the bust-up patch from 25 long years holding up Dad's ass. Now, past the old dust-covered exercise bike which does not work anymore, Jack thinks, so why is it still there?

*

Dinner is pot pie, which is really chicken noodle soup baked as a casserole, a dish Jack always thought seemed unsettled in its identity. At some point in his life, his mother decided he liked it. So, Jack ate it, never one to argue.

Good soup, Mom, Jack says.

Is it soup? He doesn't know.

Good dinner, he corrects himself.

Jasmine sifts through her noodles, stabs each slice of celery, and stacks it in a wall of brothy, soft green bricks.

Dad finishes his food. Carries his dishes to the sink. Takes two green-bottled beers out from the fridge. He hands a beer to Jack.

Jack's mother looks distressed but doesn't protest.

Jack notices. He swallows down a slow and guilty sip.

The hand that holds the bottle quivers slightly and he puts it down.

His mother is stirring through her noodles and she doesn't seem to see.

His dad turns his head to the side, a little, like he might've seen the quivering, but chooses not to say so.

Jasmine looks at her brother. Smiles timidly.

What does it feel like? She asks, gesturing to Jack's head.

You mean, my brain? Or being back here? Jack laughs gently.

She shrugs. I don't know. I mean, do you feel different?

Jack thinks for awhile. He is not sure what to say.

Like, with your memory, she says. Do you remember being here before?

I do, says Jack. I mean, I do remember being here. It's just events—specific things that happened—blend together.

She nods, like that makes sense. She starts to ask, do you have trouble...

But his mother interrupts.

He's having trouble, but he's going to get better. And we need to help him, work together, work with him, to get him better.

Jasmine shrugs. Her green brick wall begins to topple. So much celery, thinks Jack. Who even likes that shit?

His dad downs his beer. Stands up. He takes both their bottles before Jack has finished his. Jack smirks a little to himself. He thinks, that was supposed to be my chance with Dad. I guess it's over now, and I've already fucked it up.

*

Jack does the dishes. He feels weird about the process. It has been awhile since he's used a sink. He had a dishwasher—he thinks—at his apartment in Ohio, although now that he is thinking—standing at the old sink, in his old home—he does not remember.

But it feels good to foam the soap, and rinse, and get into his old routine, which feels right, now, being back here. Even if the process is a little complicated. It is hard to balance all the dishes on this tiny rack. So many choices to be made. How should he put that plate in? Straight, or sideways? Should he put that bowl in

169

first, or try to squeeze it in between the plates? And he will hover in the wake of these decisions for what probably feels like a long time—he thinks—to those watching him.

Thank you so much, his mother says.

His dad comes by and pats his back. It's good to have a man who does the dishes.

Jack shakes his hands dry, smiles awkwardly because he wishes it were no big deal.

But he knows it kind of is.

*

They sit around together, watching Wheel of Fortune.

Everyone on this show is so dumb, says Jasmine.

And it's true. Nobody seems to know you need to buy a vowel. Nobody seems to see the words through all their absences. Nobody seems to understand the concept of the show's Before and After puzzle:

J _ s t   t _ e   w _ _   _ o _
_ r e   w e   t _ e r e   _ e t ?

His mother leans over and smooths her hand along his cheek.

Do you have any...she trails off in search of the best word, here...plans?

I'd like to solve, says a contestant with a piggish-looking pink face and round glasses. And of course, he gets it wrong.

Jack says, um. I don't think so.

She keeps smoothing, searching.

The contestants keep spinning idiotically and guessing wrong.

She picks a dry flake from his face. Her nails are too sharp.

Ow, Mom! His voice comes out sounding just like it did when he was five.

And he remembers being five without remembering, just hearing something in his voice, something that never left.

*

Jack takes his medicine. Six pills.

Tonight, they taste like peeled paste.

He holds them on his tongue and gathers his saliva. Gulps them down.

He goes to bed first, thinking he should get the staircase over with. Shuffling feet that still feel heavy, still don't move the way he tells them to. His brain, so sensitive and sluggish, all at once, his thoughts—his messages to move—like screaming legs in nightmare quicksand.

His brain says: step.

He lifts his foot and flops it down.

His brain says: harder, step.

He lifts his foot and flops it down, but straight.

His brain says: stronger, step.

He lifts his foot and guides it smoothly down, at first, but something spasms, slightly, at the last second.

He does all right, all things considered, with the weak and creaky railing. He concentrates his energy on each step, which is easy because each step has a different colored carpet square.

| Square 1 | tan-pink |
| Square 2 | gray-blue |

Square 3	blue-green
Square 4	green-yellow
Square 5	red-orange
Square 6	red-brown
Square 7	peach-white
Square 8	gray-brown
Square 9	beige
Square 10	black

The squares feel rough beneath his bare feet, nubbed with age and wear, with raw, scarred edges, underneath which you can see some sort of tacky base.

Good night, Jack calls out from the summit of the stairs.

Good night, says Dad.

Good night, says Mom.

Good night, Jack, says Jasmine.

*

Jack's old bedroom is full of boxes that were piled—as much as possible—along the far wall from his dresser and his bed. There is a bookshelf and a pink desk with some drawings that his sister made, but otherwise, the old room is the same. It is the same dresser, the same bed, same plaid bedspread. Lying down, it feels the same as he remembers: thin and saggy, sunken in.

His posters were torn off the walls, but you can still see shadows from the tape, stray shreds still here and there, gray film with black grains.

Jack looks up at the ceiling full of fragmented film, feeling—

but not quite seeing—reels projected from the sticky bits. A stream of glitchy scrapes and specks of coal grit, spurts of pieces—every now and then—of pictures that were once there on the walls. A piece of someone's chin. A piece of someone's elbow, eyeball. Pictures that were once picked out—by him—and trimmed, smoothed over with his hands. These images of things that were important to him—must have been—once. In their way, still there, of course. But now, no longer seen.

*

Down in the bottom of the biggest box in Jack's room, at the far end of the stack—there, in the corner, in a cluster-fuck of trophies—is a photo album from Jack's high school days, a little remnant from the room when it was full—before—when it was lived in.

It starts in springtime. You can tell because it starts with fifteen photos of Jack and his sister—still a tiny kid, then—posed with cheesy toothy grins and ta-da hands around the Easter Bunny Cake: a whole cake head, two half-cake ears, licorice whiskers.

Then, graduation: Jack so handsome in his gown and cap, his hair—just peeking out beneath—immaculately faded. His trademark licorice-thin mustache. Tall and strong, leaning to kiss his mother on the cheek while pinching his diploma in his armpit.

Then, all his different groups of friends: all tall and strong—athletic—making stupid faces, making different faces, making faces into some wide-eyed unspoken joke about the way their faces usually were, about the way their faces had to be.

Pictures of three young men pretending to be fighting one another.

Making their cartoon-wide eyes of fear and anger.

Pictures of three young men pretending to be gay.

Making their cartoon-wide eyes of lust and longing.

Arms around shoulders and waists, shirts lifted up: a crazy joke.

Jack's body looks so good, there. Looks like he worked hard to look that good. Looks like he almost had prepared himself for just that moment. The blonde-haired white guy with a red cup, black-haired white guy making kiss-lips...who knows what they want, or what they're really thinking.

The blonde-haired white guy must be Dan.

The black-haired white guy must be Gio.

Both names, there. Black ink, on the back. Predictions of forgetting.

*

Jack stirs at 6:00 am. He hears his dad's alarm go off. The floors creak with Dad's footsteps. Groaning of the pipes. The whisper-hiss of the shower. Mom's alarm at 6:15. Floors creaking, stairs. A muffled clink of dishes, rustle-growl, a rising coffee smell. Jasmine's alarm goes off at 6:30, then quickly shuts back off, goes off again, 6:35, 6:40, 6:45.

He hears a light mist rain. A tap, tap, tap. The morning is a sad stain through the curtains, drizzling along the blonde wood-paneled wall. He hears a sizzle, smells warm butter, and considers getting up, but there's a certain pleasure to just lying there and listening. Like playing sick when he was little, lying in the light, and feeling so excited in the wrongness of the lie.

And now he is sick—isn't he?—and it's exciting to remember this so pointedly, the sensation of being young and wrong.

*

At 7:10, his mother comes in. Coffee breath and soap skin. Dangled keys, sliding a door key, $5 onto his bedside table.

I'll be back by 8. I'm at that group home in the country, now.

She says the country like they live in some great town.

She quick peck-kisses, asks for Jack to pick up something from the store.

But only if he can remember, though.

She says this with a slight twitch of her mouth, like it's a test.

And Jack resents that twitch. He promises he will.

But he goes back to sleep and dreams of flicker film, and elbows, eyebrows, fragments of dark hair, and dark eyes...

He forgets.

*

He wakes up with a start, thinking: I think I lost something.

I don't know what.

His sheets are sticking to his legs.

He rubs his eyes.

He watches dim light draining down the wood until the drain thins, slowly, and the light expands across the panels, opening, revealing nothing.

Do you have a plan?

A plan.

He rumples from the sheets, untwists his legs.

He has to tell his legs, okay, untwist yourselves, and wait for them to wake up.

And he has to tell them, okay, now shift to the bed's edge.

Okay, put your feet down.

Okay, now we need to stand.

And when he stands, his bones feel staticky, his skin some thin, charged cloth left out too long to dry, now pricked tight, ragged, tickling his nerves. Just like the ancient terry towels that he finds folded over the baseboard. Waiting for him. Like he is a guest.

*

He peels off his bedclothes, folds them, and—not knowing where to put them—lays them back over the baseboard where the towels were.

He looks down at the softened mountains of his flesh: his too-thin arms, his roll of once taut-stomach, tired blob of cock.

The mini-black hole of his belly button, frayed with threads of hair, small flakes of skin. He pinches at them with a sigh.

Yes, he is ashy, Mother. Ashen. He is ashing.

He is smoke-dry from some unseen inner burning.

He takes his medicine. Six pills in different shades of white.

He dryly gulps them down.

Today, they taste like paint. He licks his lips.

He gets into the shower, spits into the drain, stands, watching ashes of his skin become translucent shards, like glass.

*

Jack sloughs the shards from his skin, treads a little lighter down the colors of each stair: black, beige, gray-brown, peach-white.

The kitchen is a pile of dishes in the sink: the smells of dirty oil, cold coffee, and burnt strawberry Pop-Tarts. Does the dishes—takes a long time, with nobody watching—makes a pot of oatmeal, finding everything he needs. Still in the same spaces. Same shit. Same pot that has no lid, that only has one arm, that has those copper-colored singe streaks all across the bottom.

He taps the chewed-up looking wooden spoon against the pot and hums. The water boils, soaking all the oat flecks and dissolving them into a smoothly undulating quicksand, until everything is sinking into small holes going pop, pop, pop.

*

He scrapes the bowl clean with his spoon. Something about the clinking sound reminds him: drug store. I should go and get... the thing...He stirs around the empty bowl, thinking, the thing... clink clink...the thing...clink clink...the thing...clink clink...until his mind gives up.

He might as well go out. But by the time he gets the will to lace his boots, put on his coat—fuck with the sticky zipper—it's late morning, maybe early afternoon.

The sky is white-gray with the kind of winter glare that makes him feel like he is too late.

It's cold as hell. His face feels like it's getting scraped with salt. The gutters of the clapboard houses are weighed down with ice. He hears it cracking as he shuffles down the bright green astroturf. He smells it, almost: coal-cold air, the smell of lonely cold.

The sky, still misting. Wind, still blowing. And the sound of old tarps flapping hard against the many broken, open, never-finished holes.

But there are people walking up the hill, and down the hill, in wool caps, or skull caps, with their thick coats, with dingy little dogs. Or groups of teenagers somehow in nothing but their jeans, their shitty sneakers, and their hooded sweatshirts.

Mrs. Moretti sits there in her plastic lawn chair, smoking. She squints like it's so bright, like it's a summer day. Jack waves to her. She waves back, but he notices her squint gets tighter, and he wonders if she recognizes him.

*

He braces himself, shifts his feet so they are level with his shoulders.

He looks down the hill, toward the bridge to shit-creek.

His brain says: step.

He lifts his foot and flops it down.

Crr-crunch.

His brain says: harder, step.

He lifts his foot and flops it down.

Crr-crunch.

He thinks, step, step, don't slip.

He breathes in, out. Puffs of exhaust.

The crunching of each boot step reassures him he's upright.

*

Jack winds down through the streets like this, down to shit-creek, which is still there, flowing in its ever-orange, garbage-churning glory. Shuffles across the bridge, to Market Street, which smells of smoke and damp. He thinks that something very big was burned here, recently.

It doesn't take him long to find it: an entire block of red brick rubble, smashed green glass, black timbers sticking out like broken bones. The charred, warm smell that feels so wrong within the damp cold, mingled with the iron wires, like the smell of still-fresh blood.

It is the kind of thing you cannot help but stare at.

And Jack stands there, staring at it, for what feels like a long time.

He sees a metal filing cabinet.

Papers strewn around the charred ground.

Dates stamped on them.

One says February 7th, 1953.

He gets confused, then. 1953 is...not today. Already happened. This fire...burned. Before. Today is after. Not today. Today is... He looks up, around him, at the streets he's pedaled through and walked along so many times. He feels flushed. Embarrassed.

Jack realizes, suddenly, an old woman is standing there, behind him, also staring at the block of rubble. She's holding heavy bags of groceries, slumping with their weight. She has a tired, lost look Jack relates to.

They stand there for awhile, looking at the same thing, as the cold air drifts the papers, rumples through the woman's hair.

The cold air pierces through his brain.

Jack's muscles clench. He blinks.

He repeats, dumbly, in his head: 1953, 1953...

When did this happen? Jack says.

The old woman sighs.

Jack says, it smells fresh.

She breathes in. It does. It is, she murmurs. Yes.

He asks her, did the fire happen recently?

She breathes in, deeper. Before Christmas, she says. All burned down, burned down, just before Christmas.

They breathe in together, shivering.

The dust is sharp.

She coughs.

He swallows, hard.

Ah yes, she says. That was a bad day.

*

Jack shuffles from the charred black in a daze, the tang of smoke still in his nostrils, thinking, Jesus, what just happened? Looks around...okay...and he sees Benny's, Jimmy's, and Darlene's. He sees the old signs looking old and dirty, like they've always looked, as far as he recalls.

The smell of smoke begins to drift away, replaced by other smells. Red sauce and ice. Hot garlic. Garbage. Rust. Wet cigarettes. Fresh cigarettes. And suddenly, a warm hand on his shoulder from behind, a voice Jack would know anywhere, crying out: motherFUCKer!

Jack turns straight into a strong-armed hug. Gio!

Motherfucker! Jack says back.

My man, my man, says Gio. Where have you been?

Jack clutches tight to Gio's coat sleeve, breathing in his steam, his warmth, trying to press away the years they've been apart.

*

They find the nearest bar, the place that used to be Wisniewski's—which still has the same sign on the outside, same wood booths inside—but is now owned by Mike Wisniewski's son, now filled with weirdly modern lights, now featuring a backroom with restored arcade games. They've got Streetfighter, Mortal Kombat, X-Men, Ninja Turtles, all that shit we played when we were kids, says Gio, smiling big and kiddish. Gio's teeth are really white. He looks thin, fit, but maybe...off a little, somehow, though I can't think how, thinks Jack.

Yeah, I remember that, Jack sort of lies. He does remember Gio's basement. Paneled walls and darkness, left alone for hours. He does remember smells of mildew, sweat, the coils in his stomach, watching Gio bite his lip in concentration.

It's strange how everything here is the same, but different, and the differences blend badly with the crudeness of Jack's memory. The vague blurred shape of Gio slouched over the game controls dissolves into the slim, white-toothed young man who's now sitting across from him. It's dark inside the bar. The booths are filled. Stale smoke hangs in the walls, the air, mingling with new smoke, the sounds of beery laughter. The smoke stings his eyes, and he remembers, he lived in Ohio, recently, where people did not smoke in bars.

Gio lights up another cigarette and offers one to Jack, who takes it gladly—though he coughs, and Gio laughs. He rambles on about the town—the places that they used to go to, now no longer open, or no longer there. His warm voice—white teeth—curls the smoke in hazy currents as he talks about his old house, where he still lives with his mom. That's right, Jack now recalls, Gio's an only son, the only kid he knew who had no siblings.

Gio leans in, lowers his voice. Hey, so. My mom told me about...the thing...

The accident? Jack says.

Gio nods. Yeah...the accident. She said that...something happened to your brain.

Jack sucks in smoke. He nods.

They sit in silence for a minute, breathing, tapping out the ash.

*

A group of guys filters into the barroom from the arcade. Jack squints at them, thinking they look like some people he should know. One of them sees Jack squinting, squints back for a moment, claps his hands, and tugs his friends across the barroom up to Jack and Gio's booth.

Hey, Dan. Hey, Matt. Hey, Owen. Gio shoulder-slaps them as they squeeze into the booth. They dress just like they used to, same old hooded sweatshirts. Unlike Gio, though, they're looking kind of worse for wear. Thick necks with puffy chins and cheeks. Jack thinks their faces look like rough thumbs.

Dan sits with Jack, gives him a sizing-up smile. Long time, no see.

Jack laughs lightly. Yeah. Been in Ohio.

Dan laughs. Fuck Ohio.

Dan announces, beer. On me.

Okay, says Jack.

Dan leaves and comes back to the table with two pitchers.

He passes glasses around the table.

Dan takes his and fills it.

Matt takes his and fills it.

Owen takes his and fills it.

Gio fills his, looks at Jack, and pours a glass for him. He smiles.

Jack smiles timidly, takes his glass, and drinks.

*

They reminisce about the people they all knew, and mostly hated. Like Coach Novak, who had words for any player on the team who wasn't Polish. They all laugh about the time Matt made a play which prompted Coach to say, Matt Evans, you are proof that Indian fuck bull. Matt's hair is buzzed-brown, and his skin is mashed potato-white. Matt snorts, I hope that fat fuck has a heart-attack and dies.

They reminisce about the people they all knew, who are not there. Like Honeybun, the guy who earned his name by eating five family-sized boxes of honeybuns, and promptly puking on himself. Oh Honeybun, says Gio, Honeybun, we hardly knew you.

Whatever happened to that guy? Says Jack.

Gio sucks on his teeth and pantomimes a needle shooting in his arm.

*

I got two little guys, says Owen, two more glasses in. Boy and a girl. Opens his wallet, holds a photo up for Jack to see. The kids look small and weirded out. The photo's old and worn.

Jack nods. Nice kids.

He puts the photo back. They are. They are nice kids.

183

I got a little one that bites, says Matt. Bites everything. His toys, his mom, himself, he laughs. I guess it's in the genes. He bares his teeth and chomps into the air, chachachacha! He turns to Gio, chachachachacha!

Gio waves. Cut it out, you retard.

Matt's toothy noises trigger something in Jack's head. A tingling sensation builds, not pain so much as aching fog. The kind of feeling he would get from tripping with these guys, so many summers past. That nameless smell, perfuming through his brain. Jack sips his beer, thinks: this will be my last sip. Puts his glass down. Looks around the bar. His brain is fogged. Where is he? Paneled walls. Wood booths. The smoke. The modern lights. The little pinging sounds echo like cartoon sound-effects. Jack thinks, something has changed, something he can't name. Looks around the bar. The men here look the same: heavy and squarish, from the back. The men here blend together into slopes of squarish shoulders, gray smog rising, rinsing all the recognition from his thoughts.

Jack, did you hear about the shootout off of Market Street? Says Dan.

Jack shakes his head. He sips his beer, thinks: this will be my last sip.

Dan says, it's one of those things that just sums up everything around here.

Everything around here, lately, Gio says.

Dan says, a guy goes out to shoot another guy who burned him in a deal. He's fucked up, of course. He doesn't find him at the place. He finds a Mexican girl there. He shoots her, drags her to a dumpster. Leaves her there, behind it. Goes to his apartment...

Dan pauses and looks at Jack a little oddly.

Jack notices, then, his hands are twitching slightly, so he puts them in his lap.

The old apartment up the hill, by the old colliery, Gio says, trying to help.

Jack looks at him and nods.

The guy is high, says Dan. He goes home and he holds his roommate hostage, for some reason. Ties him to a chair and holds a gun up to his head. The roommate says he really has to take a shit, Dan pauses, letting everybody laugh at how ridiculous that sounds.

Jack's head feels heavy, now, with fog. Bursting with pressure. He looks down into his beer, and he breathes in. It smells like piss.

He asks to use the bathroom, Dan continues, and the guy just lets him. So, the roommate climbs out from the window on the second floor, calls the police, and there's a shootout for three hours. Roads closed off. Cops everywhere. Then, finally, they shoot him in the chest.

What happened to the girl? Says Jack.

The Mexican girl by the dumpster? Well, he shot her, Dan says. So, she's obviously dead.

But why'd he kill her? Why'd he leave her there? Says Jack.

He was high, Matt remarks, unhelpfully.

Dan shrugs like that is not important to the story.

Gio stubs his cigarette and stirs the butt around inside the ashtray for a moment, tapping at the cinders. Jack notices Gio's brown eyes have red rings underneath them. Gio glances up, and Jack looks down, like he's been caught.

The thing that's fucked up, Gio says, is that the Mexican girl didn't even live here. She grew up in town, but she'd moved out like seven years ago.

Everyone looks at Jack like they expect him to say something.

He does not know what to say.

He takes another sip of beer.

*

They tell more stories. Drink the second pitcher. Smoking. Laughing. Clapping. Shaking heads. I do remember that, Jack finds himself surprised to realize, over and over, as they tell these stories that feel both familiar and somehow so far removed from him. He is an odd shape, in the outlines of these stories, doing things they say he did and said, his brain numbly acknowledging, I did that, said that. But he feels no connection, reimagining these memories of some past Jack, some badly-acted version of himself.

Maybe I've been a shitty actor all along, he thinks. At first, he tries to follow in-line with their smoking, laughing, clapping, but he quickly tires from the effort, has to tell himself to open his mouth, breathe, to match their sounds, the stiffness of their shoulders.

Jack lets himself droop down and drift off, into some dark territory of his body full of quiet, seething steam, some inner quiet, underground space of his body from which all their movements, faces, seem like shadows cast across a curtained window.

*

At some point, Gio taps Jack on the shoulder.

Leans in, lowering his voice. Hey, how's it going?

I don't know, says Jack. It's fine.

Hey guys, says Gio, loudly, as he stands, looking at Jack, who also stands, who also claps each of the guy's shoulders in turn.

It's good to see you.

See you.

See you.

Well, see you around.

Dan says, well, its been real.

And Jack wonders what that means.

Gio heads to the door and looks at Jack.

Jack follows, wobbles slightly at the raised ledge.

Gio says, hey, hey there, watch your step.

*

Outside, the winter sky is dark. The lonely cold smell fills the air: deep, thick, and damp, and—somewhere in the distance—smoke. The Christmas lights blink. Ice hangs from the gutters, drip, drip, drip. Jack's gut feels frozen stiff. His head feels like it's leaking.

You need a ride home? Gio asks.

And Jack remembers, fuck. The thing...

He asks Gio, could we stop by the Dollar Store?

Yeah, sure.

Inside the store, fluorescent lamps buzz loomingly as Jack and Gio wander through the aisles. Jack moves slowly, trying hard to concentrate. He sees a woman running one hand through the skull caps, with the other tracing in a ghostly motion down her face. He sees a pock-marked teenager buying a liter of red liquid. All the aisles are strewn with items that do not belong there, picked up by some customer, then absently abandoned. Jack touches the misplaced items and thinks, is this what I'm here for?

Hey Jack, says Gio, in a gentle voice, the kind Jack's mother used to use when he got hurt, and she had to inspect the injury. You seem a little lost, he says. Is it—it? The thing that happened to your brain?

Jack shakes his head. My mom asked me to get one thing—one thing—and I can't do that. Can't remember what she wanted me to get.

That's easy, Gio says. It's toilet paper. That's the one thing that you always need. I promise. Toilet paper.

Jack stands in line, watching the brightly colored boxes on the black whirr of the belt, getting clawed up, and scanned, and bagged by this lady who keeps looking at him weirdly—looking at them, weirdly—batting swiftly at his toilet paper, like she doesn't want to touch it.

Jack hands the $5 to her. She counts the change in whisper voices—1, 2, 3—just like a little kid.

You from around here, she says.

Jack can't tell if this is meant to be a question, or a declaration, or a kind of strange command.

*

Gio puts the car in park on Jack's block. Whirr, whirr, whirr, the engine shivers. Jack can smell the car exhaust mixed with the coal dust from outside. Mrs. Moretti sits there in her spot, smoke drifting from her plastic lawn chair. Their porch light is lit:

a glowing cylinder of green. The green light triggers something in him, blurs of memories of evenings spent at Gio's, being driven home, too young to walk. Back when the town still felt so big. Back when their homes felt far apart. The engine, idling. The green light, sadly glowing its goodbye.

Do you like living with your mom? At home? Says Jack.

Where else would I go? Gio says. It's her and me, the bird that couldn't leave the nest.

Jack swallows. Yeah, I feel that.

But it's different for you. Gio pauses. I mean, you know. You have reasons.

Jack breathes in deep, breathes out, and watches as his breath becomes a fog. You have a girlfriend here, or anything like that?

Gio laughs. No. What about you?

Jack shakes his head.

Yeah, you know what it is, says Gio. Man, you've seen the girls around here.

Jack turns away. From his side of the car, he sees the edges of the hill, the big hill with its steeply sloping graveyard. It's dark, but he can see the jagged silhouettes of tombstones all along the iced grade, barely clinging to the ground.

I'll bet you hate it, being back here, Gio says. His breath makes clouds across the windshield and the green light gives an alien tint to his skin.

Jack shrugs.

I'd hate it, Gio says. I mean, I hate it, now.

It's just a place, says Jack. It's just the place we happen to be from.

Gio turns to him, and Jack can't tell if he's sad, or if it's just the green light, leaving sickly shadows on his face. His cheeks look hollow, and his eyes look big and dark. Jack realizes Gio's scanning him, assessing him in some way.

Do you have plans for New Year's? We're all going to The Pine Burr Inn, like usual. He sort of side smiles.

Okay, says Jack.

Gio laughs. Well, it's just a place.

They sit together, silent, for awhile.

Gio clears his throat. Do you hurt, still? I mean…does it hurt, Jack?

Jack thinks. He doesn't have the words to tell him what he feels. To do so, he would need a firm base of comparison—a then and now—and here, he cannot separate one from the other.

I still hurt some. Sometimes, he says.

Is it bad? Gio says. Like, I don't mean to pry, but I saw how your hand was shaking.

I still take pills Jack says. I mean, if that's what you mean.

Another silence falls. The engine whispers whirr, whirr, whirr.

Gio bites his lip, just like he used to when they were kids.

Jack thinks, he looks so weird and lovely in this greenish light. He wonders how he looks to Gio, if he sees the same boy—same man—or some sad sack who's been softened by his sickness.

I'm sorry, Gio says, as though he knows what Jack is thinking.

It's okay, Jack says.

I mean, I feel bad. I feel bad for you.

He pauses for a moment.

Somehow, Jack can feel the cold unfurling coil of Gio's stomach, slowly realizing what he's said.

*

Inside, his sister is sprawled out across the couch, her notebooks spread out across the coffee table, TV flashing, volume dialed down. His dad is in his old chair, and his mom is in the kitchen, heating up leftover pot pie-chicken noodle soup.

She looks up when he comes in. There you are.

He chuckles. There I am.

He puts the toilet paper on the counter. There you go.

His mom picks up the toilet paper, turns it over, and laughs weirdly.

Wish in one hand...she mutters, trailing off.

Jack finishes...shit in the other.

*

But the next night, she brings back a weird chart from the group home. It's a grid of boxes marked with 8 am, 9 am, 10 am, 11 am... through the whole day, little spaces left blank, lines to write in, little blank spaces with black velcro rectangles.

An envelope Jack opens and dumps out. A bunch of bright and simple illustrations labeled with short, simple words, like Med, Cook, Shower, Clean, Brush Teeth.

Jack balls his hand and feels his head get hot.

He says, fuck, Mom. I'm not fucking retarded.

*

Their Christmas is a cloud of comings, goings, early morning buzzing of alarms, the shriek of beaters making batter for the mashed potatoes, gravy, cakes, and cookies, all the food Jack's mom puts hours of work into, which they all eat in a 30-minute rush. She makes Jack and Jasmine pose for a photo with the cake—always red velvet, with a green iced tree and sprinkles in the middle—smile, wait, no, smile, make the hands, the hands! Jack and Jasmine look at each other knowingly. Ta-da.

This Christmas, Jasmine gets a smartphone. Jack, by default, gets her former flip phone. For your safety, his mom says to both of them. Jack also gets a cabled sweater from some nice department store, but it's too small for him because he's getting fat.

He helps his mom clear dishes while his sister curls up, tapping at her phone. His dad yells at the football game.

You miss that? Being on a team? His mother passes him a plate to dry.

Jack shakes his head, smoothing the towel in small circles.

I miss watching you with the other boys. Being a part of things. She passes him another plate, another, and another.

Motherfucker! Jack's dad spits. He smacks the chair. Jack turns to see two men colliding. He remembers that, the slamming weight of bodies knocking full force into bodies, being jolted into some space somehow far removed, yet deep within himself. He misses that, pushing his body to its limits, proving he could take a hit, that almost sick high of adrenaline. He misses having padding—armor—and a helmet, covering, concealing him, hiding his skin, his face, his body in plain sight.

How did you meet Dad, Mom? Jack says, changing the subject. I just realized, I don't remember how.

She looks down. Contemplates a spoon.

I don't know if I ever told you, she says. It was in a bar where people liked to dance, and people like your father came from out of town.

Did Dad ask you to dance? Says Jack.

I don't remember, says his mom. I do remember, though, I thought he had a good smile. I remember that he wasn't a good dancer, and that made me laugh. She laughs. It was a good night. It was nice.

She looks at Jack like she is looking for some traces of his father from that night, when everything was good and nice. It was a different town, she says, when I was young. People were strange about others, you know...others, not from around here. Even just a few towns over. Even inside the towns, the way they were divided in their different parts.

Jack turns in time to see a pack of men colliding on TV, to hear an awful, twisting crunch, a scream of pain. He sees the replay: bodies diving toward the body, pivoting its leg, and pummeling into its tender points. Crr-crunch. They lay the body out. They lift its broken parts onto the stretcher. Take the helmet off. The body turns its face onto its side—don't look at me, don't look at me—but Jack can see the dark hair, teeth clenched, dark skin, as the face ducks deep into its shoulder. The body raises an arm for the camera. Gives a thumbs up. Everybody in the crowd cheers loudly, coldly, crazily. The other players shake their heads in horror. Jack's mom shakes her fingers dry. Jack's dad hisses between his teeth.

Jack's mom hands him a knife, hilt first. She tells him to be careful with it, please. He takes the knife. He slowly runs the towel down the flat of each side—feigning great care with the dull blade—waves the towel out, and drapes it all across the dishes like a tarp.

*

Jack's mom and dad go back to work. Jasmine drifts off around the house, tapping her phone, laughing at things Jack does not see. She sounds relaxed and happy, Jack thinks, more relaxed and happy than he's ever heard her, and he wonders who she's chatting with. He wonders if he's ever met them—if he knows them, if she even knows them, if she's even met them, if they're from around here. When she is hungry, she makes peanut butter and marshmallow sandwiches, feeds Jack the parts she doesn't feel like eating. Jack takes his pills. They taste like cardboard. Taste like paper. Taste like nothing. Clicks through channels, drifting in and out of consciousness. Judge Judy. Law & Order: SVU. Flip Or Flop. Love It Or List It. Deal Or No Deal. Howie Mandel nods his bald head toward the woman on the show—a mother with a sick son, whom she mentions every time the spectral silhouetted banker in the red-lit box offers a deal. $10,000. The crowd screams. $22,000. The crowd screams. $64,000. The crowd screams and cheers, deal, deal, no deal, deal! The mother says, my sick son. No deal, no deal! So she keeps eliminating women with symbolic metal briefcases, watching the banker's offer going up and up and up, until it's too much for her, and she caves in to the offer, and Howie Mandel raises his pastel shirt sleeves and reveals: you made...not such a good deal. The news at 6. Some local witnesses describe the shootout. I heard screaming, says a neighbor. Not just normal screaming. Scary screaming. You can tell the difference between normal screaming and a scary scream, a scream that sounds like something serious. They show the house, the street, the caution tape, the dumpster in the alley where the Mexican girl was left out to die. They show a ring of lit novena candles all around the dumpster, flickering. They say they can't release any more details.

*

At night, the fragmented film plays in Jack's head, a scraped-up stream of tape-tipped edges, fluttering and flickering, sticking together. Streaks of brightly colored movement. Headlights. Shoulders. Helmets hammering. Colliding. Crashing. Bones crunching. Crr-crack. A blur. A blast. Then, black. Don't look. Don't look. No deal. No deal. Ashes. Ashes. Ashes. And we all. We all. The steam, the smell of smoke. The drifts of white smoke rising. Fading. Was it ever really there? An inner burning. You're in trouble. You're in trouble. You've been caught.

*

A cold front comes with New Year's Eve. Jack's family bundles in layers of thick coats and blankets to go to the coal drop. Just like the countdown in Times Square, except it's in this town, and instead of a crystal ball, they drop a lump of coal.

Jack takes a shower. Brushes his teeth, flosses. Rubs his face with lotion. Contemplates, then takes his dad's cologne, and sprays a little on his neck.

He takes his pills.

They taste like chalk.

He smacks his mouth.

He licks his lips.

He zips the pill bottle into the pocket of his coat.

*

Gio pulls up at 10:08, the window of his car cracked, smoking, burning vapors in the hard cold of the air.

He smiles white with tic-tac teeth.

You ready for some karaoke?

He laughs.

Jack laughs.

They both know it's nothing to get too excited for.

They drive through town, past shit-creek, farther up the mountains. Jack sees that the Christmas lights are still lit almost everywhere. For a few minutes, the lights blur his consciousness of where and when he is, and why he is with Gio, and where he is going. For a few short minutes, Jack feels—and imagines—he has never left this town, has never been apart from Gio. Maybe... even...He closes his eyes and pictures flicker film-tape images of them together, touching...one another. Maybe...maybe...But when Jack opens his eyes, he sees the tall sign for the Pine Burr Inn, the sign that says:

Breakfast - Daily - 8am
Cold Beer TO GO
HAPPY NEW YEAR

And he recalls where he is, and what they are both there for, and remembers: it is New Year's Eve.

The parking lot is full, and cars are pulled off on the road-side, on an incline, leading up the steep grade of the hill. Gio parks halfway up the hill and shuffles through the dead leaves and the ice. He holds open Jack's door. He holds his hand out.

Jack's brain says: step.

He lifts his foot and flops it down.

He stumbles forward into Gio.

Hey, hey, steady there, man, Gio whispers.

Jack's brain says: harder, step.

Gio pulls Jack toward him, using his elbow to pin Jack's arm tight up against his body.Crr-crunch, crr-crunch.

Their footsteps in the snow, moving in time.

Don't worry, I won't let you fall.

Crr-crunch.

Firm warmth of muscles pressed against him.

Jack can hear the tinny sounds of music bleeding from the bar, closer and closer, slowly drowning out their footsteps.

*

There's something so lovely—so welcoming—about the hollow strangeness of the karaoke music, red bulbs casting rosy shadows on the paneled walls, the shitty voices of the singers, who are all so obviously already fucked up. Gio and Jack push through the beery-smelling strands of bodies, still pinned tight to one another, until Dan and Owen wave them to the little corner table where they're sitting with a set of glasses and a pitcher, already half-drained. Gio sits down and pours himself a glass. Pours one for Jack and passes, watching to make sure the glass makes it to him. They make eye contact for a moment in the process. Gio's eyes are dark, dilated, sharply focused.

Jack's skin shivers.

We've got a game here, Owen says. Whenever someone gets up on the stage, we guess what song they'll sing. Whoever gets it wrong does shots.

The last song finishes. The crowd claps as a gamey-looking, stubble-faced man gets up on the stage.

Dan guesses, Lynyrd Skynyrd.

Owen snorts. You always guess that.

The song begins to play, and Dan is right.

Dan makes them all do shots of some disgusting fruity-flavored vodka.

Gio looks at Jack, holds up the shot, and grimaces.

*

A skinny woman in a heart-pink sack-dress gets up on the stage, holding another woman's hand, hiding behind her shoulder.

The Rose—Bette Midler, Owen says. He laughs. Okay, fine, I cheated. Every week, they come here. Every week, they sing that fucking song.

The first few bars play, and the skinny woman shrinks away and shakes her head. The other woman nods. She whispers something to the KJ, who restarts the song. She puts an arm around the skinny woman, stands beside her at the mic, whispering all the lines into her ear.

They always do this, Owen murmurs. Every week.

It makes the song into a triple echo chamber of the karaoke track, the woman whispering, the skinny woman at the mic:

Some say love   hisswhisperwhissswhiss   Some say love

it is a river   hisswhisperwhisperwhisss   it is a river

Gio shifts closer in to Jack. You see? He says.

Jack looks and shrugs. See what?

The skinny woman's legs begin to shake.

There's something off, says Gio. Something off about most people from around here. Like they don't know where they are. Like there's just something in the air.

Jack sips his beer. Claps loudly for the skinny woman. Takes a shot. Then, takes another shot, another, and another, because he cannot remember any names of songs or singers. Every song rings like a hum, unknown, unreachable, somewhere inside his head. One bleeds into the next into the next. He feels drunk. He starts to say something, and realizes he cannot control his mouth. His words are thick, all sticking to his tongue. He watches other peoples' mouths moving, so quickly. So amazing, this ability to open up your head, and just pour sounds into the air. So many sounds, hanging so heavily, this lonely red-lit fog of language. Gio laughs. Jack watches him, his lips moving. He tries to laugh along with him, to cover up his stuttering. His head starts humming harder, grating horribly. He shuts his eyes, and opens them, the red light blooming violent halos in its haze, the sound of strangers' laughter—chachachacha—rings right behind his eyes, now buzzing, burning, shredding, like a hot saw.

A squat, thick-necked man moves up to the stage. He has short, stiff-gelled hair, which is so shiny it gleams rose-pink underneath the reddish light. He wears a button-down with cargo pants, his pockets bulging with his keys and wallet, straining them around his thighs. A somber sweet piano melody begins to play—Stay, by Rihanna—damn, thinks Jack, I never would've thought—and then, the man grips tightly to the microphone and knits his brows together like he is about to tell the whole room something serious. His singing voice is also unexpected: deep and rich and sad. He closes his eyes, losing himself in the song. He slips into a breathy, barely-there falsetto when he sings the second verse, It's not much of a life you're living...

Gio leans in. He whispers something in Jack's ear.

Jack shivers.

Gio chuckles, softly. Well, well, well.

Well, what? Says Jack.

I didn't think you went for guys like that, says Gio.

Jack's skin burns.

No. Wait...I mean...he searches for the words he knows he needs to say...don't say, can't say the words he wants to say, the wrong words...What the fuck, he hisses. Don't say shit like that around them.

*

It is 11:55. The KJ powers down the karaoke, switches all the TV sets to Times Square. The buzzing barroom hushes to a gentle murmur as the television shouts—the New York crowd rush—overtakes them. The mic gets passed around in Times Square—Omaha! Miami! Pittsburgh! St. Paul! Indianapolis!—yell men in puffy coats. Their wind-reddened faces. Bright. A minute from the New Year, the announcer says. The camera pans up to the tall clock tower with its flashing ads. The screen counts down the final minute—49, 48, 47—2,680 crystal triangles make up that ball, says the announcer—29, 28, 27—200 new triangles this year represent the gift of harmony, he adds—25 seconds left!—a glitchy shuddering of fake, recorded clock sounds click-click-click—Now, 20 seconds! Grab someone you love!—Jack's eyes dart left to Gio. Gio laughs. He puts his arm around Jack's shoulder and fake punches him—tap, tap, tap—Pour your glasses and get ready for a toast, says the announcer—14, 13, 12—The whole bar holds their glasses up and counts out loud—10, 9, 8, 7, 6, 5, 4, 3, 2, 1! Fireworks erupt on-screen. Poppers explode with streamers in the bar. Smoke smells and sound. The KJ starts the fog machine. The red lights become streaks of pulsing pink. The whole bar screams. The KJ plays some midi version of Auld Lang Syne. Jack feels sick. His legs feel weak. His head droops down into the warm hollow of Gio's throat. Hey, hey, man, hey. Gio takes Jack's chin in between his hands and tilts it up. His eyes are dark and wide. His teeth are white. Jack mumbles something he cannot hear. Gio hisses, shakes his head. Hey. Hey, there. It's okay, man. It's okay, Gio repeats over and over, as he stands firm in the middle of the red-pink pulsing room, stroking Jack's hair, shaking his head, and looking down on him.

*

Inside his pocket, Jack's phone buzzes as his mom sends him a picture of the coal lump: just this big, dark, crappy shadow by the bank—the tallest building—in the center of their town, his little sister's mitten—silhouetted in the foreground—giving him a thumbs up.

*

Meanwhile, the scent of cold steam rises from the pop of fake champagne bottles across the town.

In other bars. In clubs.

In the Italian Club, where old men and old women sit, and look—at young men and young women—sipping sweet dessert wine, and remembering.

In the Polish Club, where young men wearing button-down shirts dance with young women wearing their thin skirts and high heels with no nylons—going click click, shuffle, swish, swish, click click, shuffle, swish—around the room, kissing with chapped lips, ruddy pink legs pricked with goosebumps.

*

Meanwhile, the warm steam rises from the vent beneath the earth—the old town—in the crevices of old walls of the old, no-longer buildings, by the old highway—beyond the view line of the new highway—beyond the consciousness—the lives—of anyone who's living.

*

When Jack comes to, both Dan and Owen are not there.

He squints against the red glow: bodies, fog, and glitchy movement.

An awful, clenched-up feeling overtakes him, suddenly, like invisible fists gripping his brain, pushing it out, holding it out above of his body. He can hear this sort of baby-whimper sound begin to build in—what he knows is—his own throat. And he can feel the red-hot flushing of his cheeks. His tears. Before they come, he thinks, fuck, Jack. The fuck. This is a bad look. Then, he's crying. Quiet baby-whimper sobs he can't hold back. A quiet baby-whimper voice he knows is his, but doesn't sound like his. This is a bad look, Jack, he thinks, over and over. Jesus Christ. This is a bad look. It's a really fucking bad look.

But somewhere through the clenched-up, held-out-at-a-distance-feeling, he hears Gio's voice over his shoulder, whispering, okay, let's get you home.

He feels his stomach shifting as he's helped up from his chair.

Outside, the ice-air stings.

The cold.

The dark.

Jack winces, stomach sloshing.

In his pocket, his pill bottle shakes in rhythm with each step.

Warm muscles, pressed against him.

Okay, step, says Gio.

Okay, harder. Step.

Okay, okay.

Jack's stomach twists to hold the burning in his gut.

Behind them, two broad-shouldered men exit the bar.

Jack feels them, looking at him.

He does not hear what they're saying.

But he hears a twinge of something in their voices that ignites something inside his brain.

The hard-cold part that grits itself for violence.

He hears them laughing.

In the distance.

Then, a few paces away from them.

He hears their footsteps crunching in the snow.

As they go down, and down, and down the hill, one footstep at a time.

Okay, now, step. Gio is whispering more quietly.

Jack hears a sharp jolt in the laughter from behind him.

There is something mocking in the voice, like it is mimicking Jack's sobs.

Jack's mouth is bile-hot.

His mind is fire.

His thoughts are sounds of sensations remembered: bodies slamming into bodies.

The steps get closer.

Harder.

Gio grips him tighter.

The laughing gets louder.

Jack feels his mouth open, slurring sounds.

Youwannasaythashittttomeyoufuck.

Gio clasps at him fiercely. Fuck, Jack.

Jack can hear the footsteps, rushing.

Hears the swishing of the coat sleeves, as he lurches.

Leans over.

And pukes.

You wanna—-uggghh—you mother—god—you wanna—ugggh god—think you're—-uggh—-you think—uggh, god, ugh, fuck—you faggot bitch.

He hears a shuffle in the snow.

He smells their sweat.

He winces, bracing himself for a hit.

He feels Gio's hand against his back.

He hears one of them mumble, Jesus, and the other laughing stiffly.

Vomit sticks inside his nostrils.

Acid pools in the snow.

He holds tightly onto his knees, hunched over, coughing.

Burning inside, outside.

From the pool, a hot sick steam is rising.

*

The car goes whirr, whirr, whirr. The trees loom. Gray. Light-frosted branches bare and gnarled. Reaching. Jack closes his eyes. He feels the dark hiss of his insides. Feels something in them—in him—like an old stick broom, sweeping the slimes and steams and seepages around the basements of his mind. He feels drained. He squints. He feels his eyeballs. Aching bulbs. The distant blurs of Christmas lights, still blinking. On, and off, and on, and off, and on, and off. He feels the cold glass of the window pressed against his cheek. He swallows sour acid. Hissing. Shifts, and realizes that the car's no longer moving. As a hand clasps at his stomach. Reaching. Glinting. On, and off, and on, and off. Pale flashes of serrated nails.

Jack looks up.

And Gio's eyes get red-wide with a look he recognizes.

You're in trouble, you've been caught.

Don't look at me, don't look at me.

Jack looks at him.

He blinks.

Jack feels hot tears in his own eyes.

Gio laughs oddly, like a set of breathy punches. Ha. Ha. Ha.

Jack tries to laugh-punch back. He doesn't know what else to do. His laugh tastes bad and bitter in his mouth. He licks his lips.

Ha. Ha. Ha.

Ha. Ha. Ha.

Gio lets out one last punch-laugh, then swallows. Looks out through the windshield. They watch the windshield as it gets fogged up with swirls of false heat. With nervous breath. A soft haze building from both corners of the glass, expanding out in waves, of winglike streaks of ghostly respiration. Gentle, trepidatious ha, ha, ha. With silent pauses. Scanning twitches. Hairs raised. Fluttered blinking. Searching hands.

The frame of fog building, and thickening, until the glass can no longer be seen through, and both sides meet—merge—together, in the middle.

*

Meanwhile, in the town, the iced-flecks of the seafoam mural crack.

The bits break off.

The shapes bleed.

No one notices.

And no one notices the parked car, idling.

And no one notices the bodies inside, moving, drifting through the fog.

*

Down in a small box—in the bottom of the inside of another box—in Jack's room, there's a set of photos no one ever looks at. If they looked at them, their memories would play a flicker film of worries, images nobody wants, no longer needs.

His sister took them, with his mom and dad both hovering and pointing, pointing out what the insurance company should see.

A close-up shot of all the bandages around Jack's head: a thick white plaster, like a shower cap made out of concrete.

The picture shows how there were red wires coming from the plaster cap. Tiny white flakes around his forehead and his eyes—which were still closed, of course—a thick triangle of some kind of medical tape holding his nose on, holding his face—somehow—together.

A close-up shot: the breathing tubes stuck in Jack's nose—two big blue tentacles of plastic from the bright blue-screened machine—two more, both see-though—leading up into suspended bags of fluid—dry frown, drooped mouth, beneath all the weight of what was keeping him alive.

Another close-up of the neck brace Jack was wearing. Such a strange shape, like the pelvis of a skeleton strapped to his collarbone. Here, you can see the slouching body in its sag of mint-green gown. The surface of the pillow that his mom kept smoothing, pointlessly.

A final shot, a long-shot, meant to showcase everything together: how the brace, the tubes, the concrete cap, how all the false parts connect. Here, in the bottom corner, you can see two separate hands—two little gold rings—pressed on top of one another.

*

But Jack still carries it.

This nothingness.

This nothing: doing nothing, feeling nothing, being nothing— in a dark part of his brain.

This hissing, hot-cold-white-black soundlessness of nothing.

There's a vent that he can visit, crawl inside, and disappear into.

*

When Jack wakes up, the room feels weird, stained with a weak gold light. And for a long time, he cannot remember where he is, or when he is. He feels so settled in this weak light—in the pilled warmth of these sheets, stuck to the curled hairs of his legs, rumpled around his curves and sharpnesses—he feels he has always been there, here, steeped in this light. He knows he hasn't, knows this feeling is some kind of lie. But when he reaches for the un-lie—the before, the after, then and now, he feels weak, and blank.

And—furthermore—he doesn't mind.

But then, he coughs. His head feels heavy, too thick for his neck. And something in the cough contains the question: Where am I? Who am I? And then he feels—without remembering—his young-wrong sick days: willing himself into softness. Into sickness. Stillness. Soft time.

He lies in bed, watching the light expand across the boxes in his room. He thinks, there. That's me. In those boxes. Little coffins of my life. He starts to wonder who and what is therefore in this bed, but he is interrupted by the footsteps creaking down the hall. And even though he starts to understand he's in his old house, in his former room, part of him honestly is not sure who the footsteps might belong to. When he sees the shadows of two feet beneath the door, and hears a gentle knock, part of him thinks, that could be anyone.

Come in, Jack says.

Jasmine opens the door, holding a plate with two strawberry Pop-Tarts. Both look and smell burnt. She puts the plate down on the bedside table. Sits down on the bed. She looks at Jack like she expects him to say something.

He sits up.

Thanks, he says, somehow. Strawberry, huh?

The best, she says.

Correction, he finds himself saying. Worst.

She shakes her head.

She picks a loose end from her braid.

She rubs the braid around between two fingers.

Licks her fingertips and smoothes it into place.

Jack, she says flatly. Mom and Dad are freaked out.

What are they freaked out about? He says.

She makes a little hiss-click sound. About you.

Jack immediately feels a rush of cold inside his chest, like Jasmine's hiss-click tapped and popped and drained his warm lie.

When you were gone til 3 am, they freaked out, Jasmine says. Mom sat right by the window, looking through the blinds like every 30 seconds. She kept saying it was 3 am, 3 am, when it happened. Like there's something magic about 3 am.

Jack rubs his head. He can't remember getting home. And for

a minute, he forgets why he is there. He thinks, what happened? What is it? But then, it comes back in a blur of blinking lights, and shitty voices, and the whirring engine, hands, and skin, and fog, and...that was real.

And then, that guy helped Dad help you get up the steps, Jasmine says. Dad said thanks, but when he left, he said to Mom, I just don't know about that boy. I just don't know about that boy. He just kept saying that, the way that Mom kept saying, 3 am, 3 am, 3 am.

Jack feels a low whirr from the back of his head—top of his spine—thinking, at first, that it's just his memory—his sense of sound—from last night, coming back to him. But suddenly, the whirr becomes a painful sort of clenching, like a phantom fist is thrusting itself all around his brain. The fist is pulsing, testing at the texture of his muscle, taunting him a little with an undulating squeeze, until the whirr builds to a roar, and all the pressure of the pulsing builds to bursting, and something in him snaps open, seeps.

He starts to cry.

Not just a sniffle. Not some easily concealed irritation, but a dripping flood of tears.

He feels his face get hot. He hears an ugly moaning in his throat. His eyes get glazed, until he looks down, sees a pool of damp.

His sister's eyes are wide, like she does not know what to do or say.

He feels bad for her especially because...he feels empty. Emptied out.

I'm better, now, he says to her.

She blinks.

He adds, I'm sorry.

It's okay, Jack? She says, like his name feels like a question.

He takes the plate of Pop Tarts.

Takes one.

Takes a bite.

He takes another bite.

He puts the plate back down.

He swallows, hard.

He slowly licks the pink grit off his gums.

You really burnt the shit out of these things.

Burnt shit is good for hangovers, says Jasmine.

Jack nods. Eats the rest, dutifully, before realizing what she's really said.

You're only...he begins to whisper-count his fingers...

Twelve, says Jasmine.

Twelve, says Jack, embarrassed. What do you know about hangovers?

Jasmine smiles sadly, like she's thinking something she can't say out loud.

A too-thick thing she doesn't want to breathe into the air.

She takes the plate and dabs small fingerprints of burnt crumbs to her mouth.

She tells him, Mom and Dad. They know about your hangovers.

*

Eventually, Jack begins to crave that bitter, paper-paint taste of his pills, and he remembers it is time to take them. But when he tells his legs to stand, his feet to step up to the bathroom cabinet, he looks, and realizes that he took them with him.

He checks the pocket of his coat. There's nothing there but scraps of old gum wrappers, nicotine dust, and a crumpled-up receipt.

He smoothes out the receipt.

It's from a 24-hour gas station in Ohio, dated and timed—2:53 am—minutes before the accident.

The receipt says:

THANK YOU FOR SHOPPING
1.85 oz TWIZZLERS NIBS
6.11 GALLONS UNLD
GOD BLESS

He looks at this receipt—at this peculiar prayer of measurements and numbers—for a long time, like it might reveal something.

*

After awhile, the receipt starts to look just like the Pine Burr Inn sign, and Jack knows that's where the pills are, where he needs to go, that he will find the bottle on the floor—still there—untouched—unnoticed—underneath the chair, where he was sitting next to Gio in the bar. He sees it clearly in his mind: red glow, wood paneling. He feels it all collected, zipped inside in the pocket of his memory. He gets dressed, pulls his coat back on, picks up, re-crumples the receipt, and he prepares to walk back through the town, and up the hill, and back through time.

*

Jack makes his slow descent, from black to beige, from beige to gray-brown, from gray-brown to peach-white, peach-white to red-brown, to red-orange. The sound of Jasmine's whispered phone-voice—hushed and serious—climbs up the stairs the opposite direction, tickling its way into his nerves.

He sees her, sitting in a worried curl down at the bottom of the stairs.

I know...

I know, Mom.

No...I said that.

No...He didn't say.

He started crying.

No. I don't know...

No.

He didn't say.

I know.

No...I don't know.

She looks up and she notices him.

She whispers, Mom, I need to go. He's out.

Jasmine rises and moves to block his way down at the bottom of the stairs. She asks him where he's going, and he struggles to explain. The story sounds a lot less logical when said out loud. It feels less logical, watching his words reflected in her face.

She doesn't protest, though. She gets her own coat from the closet. Puts it on.

A big white puffed cloud of a thing with sooty smears.

Jack thinks, it makes her look so small, and somehow, strangely brave.

She pulls her hood around her hair.

She says, I'm going with you.

*

It is an overcast day, but no clouds are visible. The sky looks flat, almost opaque, and weirdly yellow-gray. The whole sky is the color of the moon. It's like the New Year's moon got cancerous and grew somehow, consumed the atmosphere.

Mrs. Moretti sits, exhaling separate streams of smoke from both her nostrils, dirty strands of hair drizzled around her face. Jack waves. She waves back, squinting hard, and leaning forward in her chair. Less like she's greeting them. More like she's waving them away.

Jasmine walks slowly down the hill, pacing her steps in time with Jack's. She watches him. She tries to mirror all his movements.

So she does not observe the ominous red boards with their white Xs nailed to the doors of houses on the street. And she does not notice the covered stretcher coming from the back door of the high-rise. Or the dumpster, with a white cross drawn in chalk, surrounded by some water-damaged photographs, decayed red roses, and a row of bright, burnt-out novena candles.

*

And suddenly, the sidewalk gapes into a charred-brick maw: ripped-open ridges, steam still rising from the ribs of broken boards. Jack and Jasmine look on into this sprawl of rubble, like they're staring at a submerged shipwreck, or the body of a bloated whale.

Jack knows the smell, that dampened warm-cold of the smoke. But it still smells so fresh, like it just burned. Did it re-burn, somehow?

How does a fire feed itself?

Re-feed itself?

How does an emptiness regenerate?

They see these papers strewn across the ground.

Old daily records, stamped with dates.

December 2nd, 1953.

November 27th, 1956.

October 13th, 1957.

February 7th, 1962.

Old reams of fabric, strips of pale silk and floral cotton, scattered in the ash. The blackened skeletons of burnt lace. An antique map. Some scraps of blueprints for a building never built. A rusted pair of scissors. Pliers. A dried, encrusted can of paint. A box of cat gut, spilling out into dismembered wires. A broken fan. A broken lamp. A broken broom, covered in dust. An open drawer of unpaid IOUs to who knows who.

March 22nd, 1964.

April 11th, 1965.

Albums of mostly damaged photographs, vague shapes: The domed clock tower of the mill—the clock now blurred—the tall arched entrance of the high school—puffed with mold—the marquee of the theater, when it was still new, when all the windows weren't boarded up, the bulbs all still intact.

But it's impossible to separate these remnants from new layers of detritus. Shredded styrofoam, cemented in the ice. A Wendy's wrapper, flapping up against a dead, decaying bird. Crushed cans and 40s. Scattered condoms filled with frozen fluid.

The woman stands beside them. Neither of them hears her crunching footsteps in the snow, the swishing plastic of her bags.

She doesn't look at them until they look at her. She has a patient look, like somehow, she has always been here, waiting.

Did you two lose something? She asks.

She doesn't wait for their response.

You might as well have. But you might as well forget.

The fire has no memory, you know.

It leaves no memory.

The fire takes it all.

The fire takes everything.

*

They move on past this pit of piled nothings. Jasmine takes her brother's hand. She leads him up the narrow sidewalks, through the jagged slants of alleys, coal-streaked clapboard, caved-in porches, faceless angels, brown wreaths, garlands, brown-gray tinsel, brown-gray, growling dogs on chains.

The Christmas lights are going strong.

Already.

Still.

The gleaming golds are beautiful against the flat gray-yellow sky.

And as they climb the hill that curves along the edge of the old colliery, the church bells chime a warped version of Auld Lang Syne.

Around another row of houses, Jack can hear a gentle crack-crack-crackle-crack.

At first, it sounds like fast-approaching, flying sparks.

A little kid wearing a pair of snow boots and pajamas rounds the corner, cruising through the sidewalks on his big wheel.

His little pedals move so rapidly.

They start to rumble independent from his feet.

He doesn't seem to mind.

The plastic crunches over gravel, pebbles, turning ice to mist.

He picks up speed, more speed, until he's scraping gusts of movement with his wheel.

Pedals skittering.

Breath in cold clouds.

Cheeks shining.

Smiling.

Raw.

Gap-toothed.

His whole face luminous and vapor-bright.

Hello, he calls to Jack and Jasmine.

Hello, they call back to him.

Jack smiles.

He thinks, that kid looks so happy.

Open the window on the sixth floor of this high-rise. Open the window, air the smoke that has collected in this room. The old perfumes of newly polished floors. The hiss of fountain soda. Vespers. Whispers. Fresh paint. Velveteen. Clean carpet. Amber incense. The old perfumes of all these old interiors. You know the ones I mean. The shuttered memories, the sacred spaces of this town. Shuttered away from dust. Shuttered away from lonely cold. Shuttered away from mists of bodies milling quietly, submissively. I know. I know. You know already. Everybody does. They tell these stories all the time. For years. For generations. All their soiled souls swept. Coal stains bleached and rinsed. Hands cupped around their mouths. So dutifully. Hands clasped in their steepled silence. Shuttering themselves away from secreted secretions. Pills and needles. Hills of tainted tissue. Tubes of oxygen. The sacred spaces of this town. The marble floors. The molded iron bannisters. These grand spaces designed as pristine shelters, echo chambers of their wealth. Their own well-being. As reminders of their ownership. Who owns them, now? These memories, these shuttered, sacred spaces? Not the ones burned down. The ones that live behind closed curtains. Halls of objects, images encased in glass. In photo albums. Boxes. Coffins. Memories. The underground hiss. Hums of expectation. Ears trained. Eyes dilated in the dark. Eyes widened. So, so deep, here, in the layered thick. So deep, here, in the illness of anticipation. All hushed and waiting for the lights to rise.

You need to know who once was there.

In that house, up there, off the gravel-sliver road.

In that now-empty house, just down-hill from the high-rise.

In that house listed for $6,000, auctioned off online.

Bought by some stranger in some city. Sight unseen.

*

You park along the clearing, where the road turns red.

You follow—as you've been told to—the dirt path through the trees beside the graveyard.

You use the garden hose to scale down the hill, toward the open vent. Between the stones. Discarded trash. Graffiti.

You come expecting something terrifying and colossal. Boiling toxic geysers. Hot steam. Glows of underground destruction.

You come expecting evidence. Some explanation. Some summation of the sinking in, the strange decay.

You get a hill.

You get a No Trespassing sign.

You get a hole inside the ground.

You get the faintest traces of that fabled steam.

You get the faintest signs of it, the slow burning, the legendary two-hundred-year fire.

You are disappointed.

*

It's dark, now. Quiet.

Here, inside the group home where Olivia now lives, where she lies in her own bed, in her own room, under her own sheets.

The sheets are labeled with her name—O-L-I-V-I-A—in thick black marker print across the bottom and the top.

The quiet amplifies the dark. It gives a voice to all the sounds she does not hear during the day (or, rather, hears without quite hearing).

Like fluorescent lights behind the locked door, in the hall. Hmmm-mmm, hmmm-mmm. Their high-pitched frequencies, droning electric hives.

Or like the girl who lies awake, in bed, across the hall. Her not unpleasant chirping tooth sounds, sighs, and feathered breathing. Here, the air is always thick with bleach. It stings to breathe. Especially at night, when everything has just been cleaned.

It's dark, now. Quiet.

The electric hives are prickling the hairs around her face and neck.

She sees a line of light beneath the door. She doesn't want to look at it. She doesn't want to look at it. She doesn't want to look at it.

She looks down at her own night-light, the little circle pink bear with its circle eyes and circle ears and circle legs.

Hmmm-mmm, hmmm-mmm, the door light hums.

Olivia does not look up. The door light makes her sad and scared. The door light lies.

The door light will not trick her into looking.

The door light will not trick her into listening.

The door light doesn't lead to her old house.

Or to her old hall.

Or to Emily's old door.

To Emily's old room.

To Emily.

The door light is a bad light.

And Olivia has been a good girl.

Ate her dinner, milk and yellow noodles.

Kept her fingers to herself.

Pointed or signed to staff.

No hitting, biting, screaming.

Took her medicine at 8 am, 12 pm, 8 pm.

Olivia squirms underneath her sheets.

They smell like fake pink.

So, she buries her hand in her mouth.

It smells like real pink.

She listens to her mouth go shh-sss, shh-sss, shh-sss, shh-sss, shhhhhhhhhhh...

This is where we live.

For your Special Occasion,
Meeting, Funeral or Formal
Affair...

Catering
Menu

Pine Burr Inn

Restaurant - Cocktail Lounge - Motel
Breakfast - Lunch - Dinner

Route 61 Atlas
1 mile West of Mount Carmel

For reservations and
Availability...
Phone 570.339.3870
Fax 570.339.3412

Visit Us @ www.pineburrinn.com